"I DON'T `                    `
more, Adam."

His rapid heartbeat slammed on its brakes, and he swore it came to a complete halt.

Just stop coming around! It would be easier to give up breathing than to stay away from Emily. "Would you like to tell me why?"

"I don't want the kids to become attached to you, Adam, so I'm asking you very nicely not to visit us any longer."

Was she afraid the kids were becoming too attached to him, or was she afraid she was becoming too attached? "What are you really afraid of, Em?"

"Nothing." Her chin rose a notch, but she didn't meet his gaze.

"You're afraid of something, and while it might partly have to do with the kids, it's not the real reason you don't want to see me anymore." He was losing her. This heat between them couldn't be all on his side. She had to feel it too. He had to show her the heat. He was left with only one option.

He slid across the sofa and pulled her into his arms. He slowly lowered his head and brushed her lips with his own. Sweet fire blazed to life. The fire was instantaneous, consuming, and insatiable.

He could feel his arms tremble as he pulled her closer and deepened the kiss. Her mouth opened beneath his and he lost himself to the flames.

WHAT ARE *LOVESWEPT* ROMANCES?

They are stories of true romance and touching emotion. We believe those two very important ingredients are constants in our highly sensual and very believable stories in the LOVE-SWEPT line. Our goal is to give you, the reader, stories of consistently high quality that may sometimes make you laugh, sometimes make you cry, but are always fresh and creative and contain many delightful surprises within their pages.

Most romance fans read an enormous number of books. Those they truly love, they keep. Others may be traded with friends and soon forgotten. We hope that each LOVESWEPT romance will be a treasure—a "keeper." We will always try to publish

LOVE STORIES YOU'LL NEVER FORGET
BY AUTHORS YOU'LL ALWAYS REMEMBER

The Editors

Loveswept 830

White Lace & Promises:

DADDY
MATERIAL

MARCIA EVANICK

BANTAM BOOKS
NEW YORK · TORONTO · LONDON · SYDNEY · AUCKLAND

DADDY MATERIAL
A Bantam Book / April 1997

ISBN 0-553-44585-5

Published simultaneously in the United States and Canada

*Bantam Books are published by Bantam Books, a division of Bantam
Doubleday Dell Publishing Group, Inc. Its trademark, consisting of the
words "Bantam Books" and the portrayal of a rooster, is Registered in
U.S. Patent and Trademark Office and in other countries. Marca Regis-
trada. Bantam Books, 1540 Broadway, New York, New York 10036.*

PRINTED IN THE UNITED STATES OF AMERICA

OPM   10 9 8 7 6 5 4 3 2 1

This book is for anyone who has ever closed their eyes, made a wish, and blown out the candles.

PROLOGUE

Adam Young would have liked to have been anywhere but the White Lace and Promises Bridal Boutique, but luck wasn't on his side. The sad truth was, luck had been evading him for the past week. He glanced in the direction the clerk had told him his bride-to-be was and, ignoring the clerk's warning, headed for the rose-colored curtains at the rear of the exclusive shop. Feminine laughter and excited chatter came from behind the fabric barrier. Praying that he wasn't about to embarrass anyone besides himself, he pushed aside the curtain and entered the fitting room.

Stunned silence from some women and gasps from the others greeted his arrival. He kept his gaze pinned to the woman in white standing before a mirror. "Excuse me, everyone, but I need a few moments alone with Georgia."

"Sir, I must demand that you leave immediately!" exclaimed the owner.

"It's all right, Cleo. He's my fiancé." Georgia De Witt slowly turned away from the floor-to-ceiling mirror to study the sole man in the fitting room. "Could we have a moment of privacy, please."

Anxious whispers and scurrying feet answered her request.

"He's not supposed to see you in the gown before the wedding," cried Vanessa, one of the bridesmaids and the only person who hadn't fled the room. "It's bad luck."

Adam frowned at Vanessa, who immediately raised the hem of her yellow gown and left as well. As the rose curtains fell still and silence reigned in the room, he turned to the woman he was to marry in little more than a month. He swallowed hard. "You look beautiful in that gown."

Georgia raised one finely arched brow. "That's not what you barged in here to tell me, Adam."

He didn't like the way she was studying him. She had had that same look in her eyes several times during the past week, and each time he'd had the uncanny feeling that she knew his deepest secret. "No, it's not, Georgia." He glanced hopefully around the room, looking for inspiration or at least a nicer and easier way of saying what he had to say. Nothing came to him. He himself preferred the truth in all things, no matter how difficult it was. His gut told him Georgia would prefer the truth too.

Their upcoming marriage was a mistake. He should have seen it months ago. It shouldn't have taken a night of blissful passion with another woman to make him understand that marrying Georgia was wrong. Her beauty didn't inspire gut-burning desire in him. She didn't hold his heart in the palm of her hand. How could she, when he had the unsettling notion his heart was just coming alive, and all because of another woman? The last thing he wanted to do was to hurt Georgia. She was a sweet, loving woman who would one day make someone a wonderful wife. That someone was not him. He knew that now.

He moved a few steps closer. What he had to tell her wasn't meant to be shouted across the fabric-strewn room. "Georgia, I can't marry you."

Thick black lashes blinked rapidly over her china blue eyes. "Why not?"

Her cool response wasn't the reaction he had been expecting. He had braced himself for either a flood of tears or a screaming fit that would peel the wallpaper off the walls. He couldn't imagine the calm and cool Georgia De Witt shrieking like a banshee, but the vision of him ducking a few well-aimed vases had filtered through his mind. No woman wanted to be jilted the month before her wedding.

He took a deep breath and told her the truth. "I don't love you."

Her chin tilted upward, but he could detect a questioning look within her eyes. "How do you know?"

He gave her a small weary smile and waited for the explosion. "I would know."

"You've met someone else, haven't you?"

Why hadn't he noticed before how shrewd and intelligent she was? Her petite build and stunning beauty were so appealing, a man was content just to admire her and never look below the surface. He wished now that he had looked deeper. There was a lot more to Georgia De Witt than she let on. "Yes."

"Last week, right?"

He didn't know what surprised him more, that she had known all along or that the crystal vase, filled with sweet-smelling pink flowers and sitting two feet away from Georgia, hadn't connected with his head yet. "You knew?"

"You've been awfully busy this past week, and you barely kissed my cheek good night when you did manage a couple of hours for me." She studied his face, her expression thoughtful. "What's her name?"

"Emily." Considering the circumstances, he wondered for the first time if Georgia was disappointed or relieved that they had never made love.

"Emily what?"

"I don't know." He shrugged, then tried to explain better. "I seem to have lost her."

Georgia blinked up at him. "Pardon?"

"I only met her once and she didn't tell me her last name."

"Did she tell you anything at all?"

He could hear confusion and possibly even laughter in her voice. He didn't know what would be worse, being laughed at or sworn at. "I know she lives in the county, is a widow, and that she has three . . ." For some reason the last word stuck in his throat, and all he could manage to get out was a funny-sounding croak.

"Three what? Cats? Alligators? Eyes?"

Now he was positive that was laughter in Georgia's voice. "*Children*. She has three children."

Georgia obviously couldn't contain her amusement any longer, and she released a very unladylike bark of laughter just as the curtains were yanked aside and her brother, Morgan, barged into the fitting room.

"What in the hell is going on here?" Morgan De Witt demanded. "Vanessa just told me you're calling off the wedding, Young!"

As Adam grimaced at the thought of Georgia's bridesmaids all eavesdropping on their conversation, Georgia stepped between him and her brother. "Now, Morgan," she began.

Morgan gently pushed her aside. "Did you or did you not call off the wedding, Young?"

Adam gave Georgia one last look. She wasn't laughing now, and small wonder. Morgan De Witt looked ready to explode, and Adam couldn't blame him. If he had a sister, he would kill the son of a bitch who broke her heart. Georgia didn't appear heartbroken, though, only slightly miffed and curious. He would have to think about that later; right now he had a more pressing problem. He squared his shoulders and faced the man who had almost become his brother-in-law. "I called off the wedding, Morgan."

The fist that connected with his eye and knocked him on his butt came out of nowhere. He heard Georgia cry out, then all he could see was a flurry of white silk and lace as Morgan dragged Georgia from the room.

He gingerly touched his eye and grimaced. All things considered, he thought it had gone extremely well.

ONE

Adam Young parked his car directly in front of the huge run-down house and frowned. *His Emily* lived in this horror? There had to be a mistake. God couldn't be so sadistic as to make the woman of his dreams cruel enough to paint the once-grand Victorian house blue. About thirteen shades of blue!

The horizontal siding of the grand old lady was a robin's-egg blue. The fish-scale shingles covering the turret were a ghastly shade of royal blue. The porch columns were an electric blue. Turquoise paint was peeling off the decorative brackets, and a hideous shade of cobalt glared from the finial topping the turret. It was an architectural nightmare, and he should know. He was one of the county's leading architects. There had to be a mistake somewhere.

He glanced at the letter lying on the seat next to him, and his frown deepened. There wasn't a mistake. This was the address the private detective had given him. He picked up the Polaroid snapshot on top of the letter and studied the woman for the hundredth time since yesterday. It was Emily. His Emily. She looked totally different from when he had met her two months ago, but he would have known her anywhere.

The detective he had hired had had very little information to go on. All Adam had known was her first name, that she had lived her entire life in Lancaster County, and that she was a widow with three children. But the one clue that had led the detective to her was that during their one night together, she had told Adam that her sister was a nurse at Lancaster General Hospital. It had taken the detective seven weeks to find Emily, seven long and frustrating weeks, but at last Adam was going to see her again.

All he needed was the courage to get out of the car and approach her door, and the wisdom to know what to say. What did you say to a woman you had spent the night with, only to discover her missing from your bed when morning arrived?

When he had stepped out of the bathroom that morning to find her gone, he had wondered if he was losing his mind and had only imagined Emily and their night together. She had been everything a man dreamed about: gorgeous, sophisticated, sexy. With one look, he had known she was special. Then when her gaze had met his, he had felt as if someone had fired a cannonball into his gut. He had swiftly crossed the crowded lobby of the hotel, where he had been a guest speaker at an awards banquet, and asked her to dance. She'd hesitated, then had said yes, and he'd led her into the lounge where soft music was playing.

After three slow dances, he hadn't been able to stand it any longer. Everything about her was driving him crazy. The way she felt in his arms, the enticing scent of her perfume, and the way her breath caught every time their eyes met. Call it fate, destiny, or just plain stupidity, considering it was the nineties, but he ended up getting a room and spending the most incredible night of his life with a woman he had just met and whom he knew only by her first name. *Emily!*

He glanced again at the photo, which had been taken two days earlier at ten o'clock in the morning. Where was the sophisticated lady that had satisfied his fantasies? This Emily was standing between a minivan and a full shopping cart, unloading bags of groceries.

She was dressed in a white T-shirt printed with tree frogs, and a pair of navy blue shorts. Her brown hair, which had been down the night he had met her, was pulled up into a ponytail, and he could detect some golden highlights under the glare of the sun. She was the picture of the perfect suburban housewife. Was this the real Emily, or was she the woman who had made his body burn time after time?

Adam slowly placed the photo back on the seat, took a deep breath, and got out of the car. He was never going to get any answers sitting there. It would have been easier to call her, but she might have hung up. She had, after all, disappeared from the hotel room while he had been taking a shower. Either she had something to hide, or she got her jollies from one-

night stands, which he doubted, or she'd been embarrassed, which seemed more likely. She'd seemed just as
dazed as he had been. He had never done anything
quite so impulsive before. In all likelihood, she hadn't
either. He didn't want her embarrassment driving
them apart, before they had a chance to get to know
each other. Their one night together wasn't enough.

Adam stepped over a raised portion of the sidewalk, where a tree root had cracked the concrete and
pushed it upward. The tree-lined street looked quaint,
but the sidewalks were a hazard. Every yard in the
once-prestigious neighborhood was overgrown with
trees, shrubs, hedges, and flowers. Emily's home
wasn't the exception.

Four massive maples fronted the yard. A boxwood
hedge that looked older than the house had been cut
back to twigs and a splattering of leaves. Three and a
half feet high, it encircled the front yard. Wisteria,
with its gnarled branches, climbed the porch posts and
overran the upstairs balcony. The stagnant summer air
hung heavy with the scent of flowers and flowering
bushes. A marble birdbath stood in the center of the
horticultural dream—or nightmare, depending on
one's view. It contained a few inches of water, two
blue and yellow plastic boats, and a Barbie doll floating facedown. He counted at least a dozen butterflies
fluttering around the overgrown perfume factory.

He made his way up the walk and onto the porch.
He knew Emily hadn't planted the miniature jungle.
Most of the plants and trees had to have been planted
long before Emily was even a twinkle in her father's

eye. Hell, judging by the size of some of the trees, he wouldn't doubt if they were part of William Penn's original woods.

Old rattan furniture with plump, faded pillows crowded the front portion of the wraparound porch, along with a red tricycle, a bucket overflowing with seashells, a stuffed floppy-eared bunny missing one eye, and about a dozen houseplants. Huge, monstrous houseplants that looked like they'd been seedlings when dinosaurs roamed the earth. He brushed a branch from an eight-foot fig tree out of his way and knocked on the front door.

He admired the cut-glass design in the oval window of the door and knew it had to be the original front door. Craftsmanship like that was a thing of the past, unless one could afford it, and judging by the paint job on the house, Emily couldn't afford it. He frowned at the wire sticking out of the spot where the doorbell buzzer should have been. Someone had wrapped black electrical tape around the ends of the wire to prevent anyone from being shocked.

When no one answered his knock, he tried again, louder. Still no answer.

Adam cocked his head and listened. He couldn't detect any noise from the house, but he could hear what sounded like children's laughter coming from the backyard. Shrugging, he headed around the porch. He had to fight his way through another jungle of giant houseplants, more cushioned rattan furniture, a child's plastic picnic table with benches, and a wagon full of rocks.

When he got to the end of the porch that over-looked the backyard, he came to a sudden stop. The children's shouts and laughter had been growing with each step he took, but he had been too curious about everything that was on the eight-foot-wide porch to pay much attention to the noise. Now he wished he had.

The backyard was overrun with children. There had to be at least a hundred. Well, maybe that was exaggerating, it was more like two dozen, but the commotion they were making made it seem like more. There were children everywhere!

Children sitting at two picnic tables, children chasing one another with water guns, children up in an old oak tree where he could barely see the framework of a tree house, and children playing with balls, balloons, and a huge furry creature that he had to assume was a dog. In the center of it all was Emily. *His Emily!* A frazzled and beautiful Emily making her way through a group of children, carrying a birthday cake.

She simply stole his breath away.

He stood in the shadows of the porch and watched as she lit the seven candles on top of the cake and the children came from every corner of the yard to sing "Happy Birthday." He couldn't tell which child they were singing to, only that the lucky birthday boy was named Jordon. He watched as a young boy leaned over the cake, paused—no doubt to make a wish—and blew out the candles. Everyone applauded and cheered. Emily beamed with pride and love. Jordon had to be Emily's son.

He noticed there was another woman in the yard, videotaping the activities. He could see the family resemblance between her and Emily, and he wondered if this was the sister who was the nurse at Lancaster General. After a minute the woman put the camera down and went back to flipping burgers and hot dogs on the gas grill.

He debated whether he should leave and come back later, but immediately dismissed that idea. He had been waiting long enough to find her. The fact that he'd arrived in the middle of her son's birthday party shouldn't be a deterrent. After all, it would be awkward for her if she tried throwing him off the property in front of all these little kids. He looked again at the birthday boy. He had known Emily had three children, but he hadn't given them much more than a passing thought. What he knew about children could be summed up in three little words—*Don't have them.*

"Hey, Jordon, what did you wish for?" cried one little kid. Another quickly joined in the friendly badgering. Everyone, it seemed, wanted to know what wish the boy had made.

Emily's laughter captured his attention and tugged at his heart. He had never heard such a sweet sound. "Don't tell them, Jordon," she cautioned as she sliced into the cake.

"Why not?" asked the brown-haired boy.

"It's bad luck. If you tell someone your birthday wish, it won't come true."

Jordon frowned at the slice of cake his mother handed him. "Really?"

"So the saying goes." Emily winked at her son and returned her attention to the cake.

Adam tried to remember what he had wished for on his seventh birthday, and couldn't. Being the only child of a wealthy couple, who had been well established in their careers and quickly approaching the end of the childbearing years when he'd come along, he had lacked for nothing. He'd had the best of everything money could buy. The best nanny, the best toys, and the best education. He had had everything but his parents' time.

Judging from the wondrous and contented glow on Jordon's face, he would say the boy lacked for nothing, including Emily's time.

"Are you a stranger?" Adam started in surprise. He had been so busy studying Emily and Jordon that he had failed to see the little girl who had just wiggled her way out from under an overgrown lilac bush at the side of the porch. She was wearing a pretty pink dress that at one time must have been clean. Now it was covered with dirt, ketchup, and some strange green sticky stuff. Both of her knees were scabbed. The lace around the top of one of her white socks was ripped and trailing behind her scuffed shoe, and he could count at least three leaves caught in the thick blond braid hanging down her back. She had a miniature version of Emily's face. Even the eyes were the same soft green. This had to be Emily's daughter.

"I might be a stranger to you," he answered, "but I'm a friend of your mother's."

The girl studied him for a few moments before smiling. "Did she invite you to my brother's party?"

"No." His gut gave a funny little lurch. She had Emily's smile too. "I happened to be in the area and I thought I'd stop by to visit."

"Oh. . . . That's okay, then." She reached under the lilac bush and pulled out a dirty doll with tangled hair. "Mom says the more the murrier."

"It's 'merrier.' "

"What's murrier?"

"The saying is 'The more the merrier.' " He considered the dirty-faced little girl and the filthy doll and wondered what the intriguing pair had been doing under the bushes.

"That's what I said." She turned to go, took three steps, then turned back toward him. "You coming?"

Adam grinned. He had just been officially invited to join the festivities. "Sure." He stepped off the porch and held out his hand. "My name is Adam Young." He ignored the dirt streaked across the back of her hand as he gently shook it. "What's yours?"

"Sam."

"Sam? Your mother named her beautiful baby daughter Sam?"

"Mom named me Samantha Elizabeth Mary-Ellen Pierce." The comical frown pulling on the child's face almost made him laugh. "I only answer when someone calls me Sam."

It took a lot of willpower to keep the serious

expression on his face. "I see." He glanced at the party going full swing all around them. No one else had noticed him yet, and Emily appeared to have disappeared back into the house. "Would you like to introduce me around, Sam?" Did one mingle at seven-year-olds' birthday parties? he wondered. And if so, what did one talk about?

"Okay," Sam said, and led the way into the mayhem.

Adam shuddered as a stream of cold water soaked the back of his white polo shirt. He quickly turned around and scowled at the two boys holding plastic water guns. Both boys giggled and ducked behind the huge oak supporting the tree house. So much for his desire to look neat and presentable when he met Emily again. His shirt was now plastered to his back, and little Sam had left behind something sticky from their handshake.

He nimbly dodged two human tornadoes covered in white frosting, cake crumbs, and spilled soda as they ran past, one shouting, "Tag, you're it!" As he followed Sam through another mass of sticky-fingered children, he considered going home, taking another shower, and starting over tomorrow.

"Hey." Sam's dirty hand tugged at his slacks. "This is my aunt Charmaine."

Adam turned and faced the woman standing in front of the grill. She was definitely related to Emily. He gave her a friendly smile, lifted his right hand, scowled at it, and quickly dropped it. "Sorry. I'm Adam Young, a friend of Emily's."

Charmaine's look went from welcoming, to curious, to a downright know-it-all grin. "I'm Emily's sister, Charmaine Beaufont." She glanced at the patio doors at the back of the house, and her grin widened. "Any friend of Emily's is a friend of mine."

Adam grinned back. He had an ally already. "Nice to meet you."

"The pleasure is all—" Charmaine was distracted by the noise of the screen being slid open. Emily appeared, balancing a tray that was loaded down with what appeared to be about thirty paper cups filled with soda or punch, and she was watching where she was going, not the party guests.

Adam breathed a sigh of relief as she safely maneuvered through five kids fighting over balloons and around the hairy dog, who was spread-eagle on the slate patio soaking up the sun. He shook his head in amazement as she reached one of the picnic tables, about six feet away from where he was standing, and carefully lowered the tray without spilling one drop.

"Is the second round of hamburgers ready yet, Char?" she called. She turned around to look at her sister, then froze.

Adam watched as every ounce of color drained from her face, and wondered if she was going to pass out. He hoped not. "Hello, Emily."

She opened her mouth to say something, but quickly closed it again.

For a moment he feared she had forgotten him, forgotten his name. "It's Adam. Adam Young."

Heat flooded her cheeks. "I remember." She grimaced as a group of boisterous boys surrounded the table and fought over the drinks. She moved away from the table and faced him. "Why . . . I mean how . . . what . . ."

Charmaine quickly stepped in between them. "Look at the time," she declared, making a show out of looking at her watch. "I have to be going or I'm going to be late for my shift."

"Go?" Emily exclaimed, clearly dismayed by the possibility of being left alone either with him or the pack of miniature terrorists. "Who's going to help me feed this crowd?"

Charmaine thrust the greasy hamburger flipper into his hand. "Adam already volunteered to stick around for a while and help you." She smiled at her sister, then at Adam. "Didn't you, Adam?"

"Uh . . ." He saw the amused gleam in Charmaine's eyes and knew she didn't have to leave right away. She was offering him an excuse to stick around. He grabbed onto it with both hands. "Yes, I did. I was just telling Charmaine how much I would like to . . ." He glanced at the spatula and then at the grill, where smoke was billowing out all four sides of the closed hood. ". . . cook." He opened the hood, choked on the cloud of smoke, and immediately flipped the burning burgers.

"See, everything is under control." Charmaine leaned forward and kissed her sister's cheek. "I'll call you later." She gave Adam a saucy wink. "Nice meeting you, Adam. I'll be seeing you around."

He grinned as he started to turn the dozen or so

hot dogs. "I'm sure you will." He liked Charmaine and owed her a debt of gratitude. He was here with Emily and there was no way she would be asking him to leave anytime soon. She needed his help. He didn't know too much about grilling hamburgers and hot dogs, but he knew enough not to let them burn. This wasn't exactly how he had hoped this afternoon would turn out, but it was a beginning.

Out of the corner of his eye he watched Emily watch Charmaine leave. She didn't look too happy about having him for her only adult company. He wondered if it was him, or because she was embarrassed. He would have to have been blind not to have noticed the tide of red that had flushed her cheeks. He hadn't come here to embarrass her, but he wasn't about to leave.

"These look about done, Emily," he said. "Do you have something I could put them on?"

His voice seemed to snap her out of her daze. "Uh . . . sure. I'll be right back." She hastily disappeared back into the house.

He turned off the grill. Every available inch of the two metal racks was taken. There had to be enough burgers and franks to feed even this rambunctious crowd. And this was the second round. He glanced down as a child tugged on his pant leg. "Yes?" Smears of white icing joined the dirt Sam had left behind.

"Dog." The small boy, whom Adam guessed was two or so, wearing a red T-shirt with *Winnie-the-Pooh* printed across the front, tugged once again on his pants. "Dog."

Adam pointed to the far end of the patio, where the hundred-pound hair ball was still soaking up the rays. "There's the dog." At least he hoped it was a dog. Its hair was so thick and long, he couldn't get a good glimpse of its face. It appeared to be snoring.

The boy tugged harder, and this time his voice was louder, more demanding. "Dog."

Adam was just about to point out the canine once again when Emily hurried from the house carrying a tray loaded down with rolls. She handed the tray to Adam and scooped up the little boy. "He wants a hot dog, not Wellington."

"How can you tell?" He glanced at the boy straddling Emily's hip. This must be her third child. Only the boy's real mother would have picked him up in his current sticky condition.

"Christopher loves hot dogs. He would eat them at every meal if I let him."

Adam shuddered and tried to remember the last time he had had a hot dog. He couldn't. He watched as Emily forked a hot dog and lightly blew on it. His gaze was riveted to her mouth and his gut clenched at the way her lips puckered. The things she had done to him with those lips should have been illegal. Desire slammed into his body like a head-on collision.

It took all of his willpower, but he managed to look away from Emily's tempting mouth. This was not the woman he remembered from two months ago. This Emily was a mother holding one child and surrounded by dozens more. He had to put this Emily, standing in the bright sunlight of the day, in context with the Emily of the night.

What better way to cool his body's reaction to her presence than to think about her children. He nodded at the boy who was reaching with both hands for the hot dog. "I take it he's your son?"

"Oh, I'm sorry." She tested the hot dog with her finger before handing it to the boy. "Adam, this is my son, Christopher." The little boy grinned with delight and bit into the hot dog. He gazed curiously at Adam as he chewed. "Christopher, this is Adam. He's a . . ."

She hesitated, and Adam mentally supplied some descriptions. *He's my lover. He's the most incredible man I ever met. He's the man I've been dreaming about for the past eight weeks.* Any of those would have done nicely. He smiled at the little boy and supplied the word Emily was searching for. "A friend."

She looked at him as if to say that wasn't exactly what she'd meant to say. "Yes, Christopher, Adam is a friend."

Christopher smiled at Adam. "Like Pooh?"

"Yes, darling, like Pooh." She lowered the boy back down to the patio. "You go play now. Remember to stay in the backyard."

Christopher waved his half-eaten hot dog and ran off.

"I think I was just insulted," Adam said with a rueful chuckle.

"When?" Emily asked.

"I was just compared to poo. You don't find that a bit offensive?"

She grinned. "He was referring to Winnie-the-Pooh, not that poo!" She opened a hamburger bun and waited for him to fill it.

Adam matched her grin as he scooped up the first burger and placed it on the bun. "I'm relieved to hear that, Ms. Amelia Carmela Beaufont Pierce."

She looked shocked to know he knew her full name. "How did you . . ." Her question died on her lips as she noticed Jordon had joined them at the grill.

Adam followed her gaze and smiled at the birthday boy. The boy didn't return the smile. He just stood there wearing the most peculiar expression. It was a toss between seeing a ghost and finding out there really was a Santa Claus.

Emily shoved the tray of rolls at Adam and stepped closer to her son. "Jordon, honey, are you okay?"

The boy blinked his brown eyes. "I'm fine, Mom." He continued to stare at Adam as if waiting for something magical to happen.

Adam shifted his feet and answered Emily's questioning look with a shrug. He had no idea why the boy was looking at him like that.

Emily shrugged too. "Jordon, I would like you to meet—"

"I know who he is," the boy said.

"You do?" Emily said.

"You do?" Adam asked. He'd never seen the boy before in his life.

"Yes." Jordon beamed. "He's my birthday wish."

"Your birthday wish?" Emily glanced between Adam and her son.

"Yep."

"What exactly was your birthday wish, Jordon?" Emily asked with obvious reluctance.

"I wished for a dad," replied Jordon.

TWO

Emily stared at her son, a feeling of helplessness washing over her. "You wished for a dad?"

"Dad?" Adam seemed to choke on the word and turn three shades paler.

Emily looked from Adam to her son and sighed. It had been a long and tiring day so far, and it wasn't even half over yet. The last thing she had been expecting was Adam Young showing up in the middle of her son's birthday party. And the last thing she needed was her son mistakenly thinking Adam was there to fulfill some birthday wish.

She knelt down in front of Jordon and wondered how long he had had this wish of acquiring a dad. Why hadn't he said something before? She didn't want to discuss it with Jordon in front of Adam. The man had too much of a strange effect on her mind, as well as her body! She gently laid her hands on her son's shoulders. "Jordon, sweetheart, you had a father. His name was Raymond Francis Pierce."

"He's dead." Jordon ignored her gaze and stared hopefully at the man standing behind her.

"Yes, he died, Jordon, but he will always be your father." She didn't like her son's belligerent tone. She wondered if all the anger she had been prepared for when Ray had died was finally surfacing.

"I didn't wish for a different father. I wished for a dad." Jordon nodded at Adam. "You can have as many dads as you want."

Annoyed by the simple idiocy of that statement, Emily asked, "Who told you that nonsense?"

"Shane Gallagher. He's already had four different dads."

Emily groaned. Leave it to one of her neighbors, Mitzi, to stir up another controversy. The woman thought it was her obligation to keep their small neighborhood in the town of Lititz guessing what her last name was. She had already gone through four different husbands, and if the current rumors were correct, number five had already been marked and Mitzi was aiming for another bull's-eye and a trip down the aisle. Mitzi had a strange philosophy of life: So many men, so little time.

Personally, Emily couldn't care less what Mitzi did or with whom, but she was beginning to be concerned for Shane and his two half sisters. The effects of their unstable homelife were showing. She glanced over to where Shane was leading an assault of the water guns on a group of unsuspecting children and shook her head. No stepfather at all for her children was better than what Mitzi was subjecting her children to. She couldn't imagine putting her own three children through such emotional upheaval.

"Jordon." She lowered her voice to a mere whisper. "I think we should discuss this later when I don't have company and you don't have a backyard filled with friends."

Jordon continued to stare at the man for a long moment before turning his attention to his mother and nodding. "Okay."

"Fine." She stood back up and took the tray of filled hamburger and hot dog buns from Adam. "Now, I would like to introduce you to a *friend* of mine, Adam Young."

Adam stepped forward and held out his hand. "Hello, Jordon. Happy birthday."

Jordon hesitantly shook the outstretched hand. "Thanks." He chewed on his lower lip for a moment, then released Adam's hand. "Are you going to be around for a while?"

"Yes, I told your mom I'd help out."

"Good." Jordon nodded again, then melted back into the swarm of kids.

Emily wished the ground would open up and swallow her whole. But just like Jordon's birthday wish, however, some wishes would never come true. She was condemned to spend the next hour or so in the company of Adam Young, the man she had been fantasizing about for the past two months. Heck, if all she had been doing was fantasizing, that would be manageable.

But she had done more than imagine being his lover, she had become his lover! If her memory served her correctly, they had done it twice. Two heaven-moving, body-shattering, mind-blowing times. And her memory was correct. All she had to do was close her eyes and she could recount every second of that night in vivid detail. The memories had been torturing her dreams for weeks.

She didn't need Adam standing in front of her to remind her of what they had shared, and what they would never share again. What they couldn't share again. Their one night together had been one of those perfect fairy-tale meetings that fill the big screen and sweep movie viewers into the vortex of passion. Into the romance.

In the cold light of day, she knew it couldn't last. She wasn't Demi, Michelle, or Meg, and Adam wasn't Mel, Kevin, or Tom. They were just two average people who happened to have been victims of a hormonal overload. She was determined that would not happen again, no matter how tempting it was. She wasn't alone in the world, free to cast her sails in whichever direction the wind was blowing. She had three children who depended on her, not only emotionally and financially, but morally too. How could she have done those things with Adam, a virtual stranger?

There was a secret part of her that was thrilled and excited that he had taken the time to find her. But the sensible mother part of her knew he had to go back to the realm of fantasy. She had seen his strained smile and the way the color had drained from his cheeks when Jordon had mentioned wanting a dad. She was amazed the poor man hadn't run for his bachelor hills. It was a heartless thing to do to a man, but anyone who had spent Lord knows how much time tracking her down needed a big deterrent. She had three.

She smiled at Adam and pulled out the last of her big guns. "You still haven't met my *third* child, Samantha."

His answering smile told her he knew exactly what she was up to. "She likes to be called Sam."

"You met her?" Emily felt her smile fade. By all rights the man should be screaming in pure terror at the prospect of spending any time with her three children. "When?" She glanced around the yard looking for her five-year-old daughter. She spotted her wriggling her way in between two honeysuckle bushes, where the children had discovered enough room to make a secret hiding place.

Last summer she had been tempted to either dig up the bushes or prune them to within an inch of their lives, the same treatment she was contemplating for the entire yard. The children had very vocally rebelled. The overgrown yard was their imaginary forest where bears and dragons roamed, or a dense jungle where lions were still the king, or a war-torn battlefield. To tame the yard would be like killing their imagination. She couldn't do that to her children, but something had to be done before the state declared her home a wildlife refuge.

"Sam spotted me up on the porch and invited me to join the party," Adam answered.

"She talked to you?" Had all the lectures she had given her children about talking to strangers been for nothing? It was an unsettling thought.

"Yes, but she wanted to know if I was a stranger first."

Emily frowned. "What did you tell her?" She was encouraged to hear that Sam at least had been listening to her lectures, but asking a strange man if he was one wasn't what she had been hoping for. Any child-molesting pervert could have easily lied to the little girl.

"I told her I was a stranger to her," Adam said, "but I was a friend of her mother's." He reached across the picnic table and righted a ketchup bottle that someone had knocked over. "She said that was okay then and that I could join the party because you always told her the more the merrier."

She placed the tray of hamburgers and hot dogs onto the table and watched in amazement as a horde of children descended out of nowhere to nearly pick the tray clean. One lone hamburger and two hot dogs that looked sadly mistreated were all that remained on the tray. "In this case, I would have to say that we should be having a merry old time."

Adam grinned and once again stood the ketchup bottle back up. "Is that the same thing as asking if we're having fun yet?"

"Children's birthday parties aren't supposed to be fun for the adults. We're supposed to live through them, take two aspirin when they're done, and swear we will never have one again." She gathered up six paper plates, all containing smashed, mutilated, and half-eaten cake, and tossed them into the trash can.

"How many times have you sworn never to do it again?" Adam asked as he cleaned off the other picnic table.

Emily smiled. "About three times a year." She glanced around the backyard and wondered how a simple birthday party for a few friends had gotten so out of hand. Easy. She had a hard time saying no to her children. She had read plenty of books on the subject and knew exactly what she was doing. She was overcompensating for the loss of their father. No mystery there.

Last Thursday had been the last day of school, and Jordon had wanted to invite his entire class to his party, as well as the new friends he had made in the neighborhood. She hadn't been able to refuse. She had been so pleased with the way Jordon, Sam, and Christopher had handled the move here last August that she had agreed with Jordon's pleas to invite *all* his new friends.

By the look of the backyard, Jordon was one very popular guy. She knew come February she would be holding the same kind of party for Samantha, only inside the house instead of outside. Samantha would be starting kindergarten in the fall and would probably want *her* entire class to come. With a weary sigh she recalled she had just signed Christopher up at the local YMCA for their Tumbling for Tots and Tadpole Swimmers Club. So much for the era of small, intimate family gatherings for the children's birthdays.

Nowadays the adult relatives stayed away and little friends showed up in droves.

Adam cringed as he picked up a paper cup and glanced inside it. His nose wrinkled with disgust, and he tossed it and three others into the trash. "Are they all this messy?"

Emily frowned at a pinecone with six plastic forks stuck into it and pitched it into the can. "This is nothing. You should see what they can do to the inside of a house."

"You let them in?"

She chuckled at his look of horror. "It's not a question of letting them in. It's a question of how do you keep them out."

Adam's reply was lost in the commotion breaking out near the base of the old oak tree. Shane Gallagher's voice vibrated through the backyard. He was yelling at a group of girls. "You can't come up! Girls aren't allowed!" he proclaimed as he leaned against the ladder, the only way up to the tree house.

Emily frowned, tossed the cups in her hand away, and headed for the disturbance. Shane was wearing the same superior look Dad Number Four had worn every time she had seen him. The boy had obviously picked up some very disturbing traits from his assorted fathers. No wonder the eight-year-old was turning into a holy terror. The sad truth was, it wasn't the boy's fault. Mitzi was always so busy satisfying her own needs, she ignored the needs of her children. Shane was losing friends all over the neighborhood, and she had heard that at least a couple of neighbors wouldn't let him play with their children any longer. Emily refused to do that to the boy, but it didn't mean he could act any way he wanted to while he was at her house.

She joined the group gathering around the tree and looked at the girls standing there. "Is there a problem?"

"Shane won't let us up into the fort," a girl with red hair and freckles said. Her black patent leather Mary Janes tapped harder with each word she spoke.

Emily bit the inside of her cheek to keep from laughing. The little spitfire looked ready to take Shane apart. She turned to Shane. "Is this true, Shane?"

"They're girls." He made a scrunched-up face and glared at the girls as if they were the lowest form of insect known to man. "They should be playing with baby dolls, not listening to our secret plans."

"First off, Shane, girls don't have to play with dolls if they don't want to. Second, this is a birthday party, so there shouldn't be any secrets. And third, if the girls want to go up into the tree fort, they are allowed. This is an equal opportunity household." She wasn't sure Shane would know what equal opportunity meant, but she was more than willing to explain it to him.

Shane looked aggravated at first that he wasn't going to get his way. Then he looked confused, as if he wasn't sure about this equal opportunity stuff. Then he looked at Adam, who had joined them, for support. When all he received from that man was a raised eyebrow, he gave up. "Who wants to play in that stupid fort anyway? When my mom marries Paul, he'll build me a bigger and better one than that." The boy marched off in a huff.

Jordon, who had silently joined them, glanced between his mother, Adam, and Shane's retreating back. Emily could almost see the little wheels in his head turning as his gaze fixed on Adam. *If he became my dad, he'd help me fix up my fort.* Emily knew Jordon wanted a better tree house, but she considered him lucky to have this one. The people who had rented the house for several years had built the tree house without permission. When she and the children had moved in, her father and Charmaine had performed a couple of minor repairs and pronounced it safe for Jordon. She, on the other hand, had stayed on the ground and gnawed at her fingernails. She was terrified of heights. It would take a miracle for her to climb those ten rungs to the tree house. In all good conscience she couldn't ask her sixty-year-old father to climb back up there and help Jordon improve his fort to his expectations. It was enough that Charmaine or her father made periodic inspections for her.

She glanced at Shane and frowned as he took a water gun from another boy and aimed it at Wellington. The poor dog was about to be rudely awakened. It was a good thing Wellington was an easygoing, kid-loving dog. Nothing fazed the dog, especially not a few squirts from a water gun. She wasn't worried about Wellington, he could take care of himself.

She was more concerned with putting a quick end to this nonsense about Jordon believing that Adam was some birthday-wish dad. Just as soon as she delivered all these kids back into their own mothers' care, she'd have a heart-to-heart with Jordon. Adam would be leaving with the rest of the party guests, Christopher was due for a nap, and Sam could easily be persuaded to spend a half hour or so playing in the backyard.

She glanced at her watch and sighed with relief. The parents should start arriving any minute to collect their little darlings.

Adam watched as Emily checked her watch. Was she hoping that the party would be over soon, or was she expecting someone else to arrive? She was as nervous as a patient needing a root canal, who had just been informed the dentist was ready. Was it because of him, or was there another reason behind her anxiety? What he knew about Emily and her life here in Lititz wouldn't fill a hat, let alone satisfy his curiosity. Maybe there was already a man in her life. He glanced at Jordon and scratched that idea. If Emily was already seeing someone, wouldn't Jordon have wished the illustrious daddy role on him?

It made sense to Adam, but as little as he knew about Emily, he knew even less about kids and how their minds worked. Maybe Jordon didn't like this fellow Emily was seeing, or maybe he just didn't class him as a potential daddy. Boy, was Jordon way off the mark by thinking Adam himself would make a good dad. The last thing he would ever be was daddy material.

The nicest thing he could do for Emily and her family was leave. He didn't belong at boisterous birthday parties. He didn't like grubby smudges all over his clothes. He hadn't known what her youngest child had been saying to him. Hell, he didn't even know why he was there. He looked over at Emily, who had just swooped up Christopher before he grabbed the last hot dog from the tray, and knew why he was there. He was standing in her jungle-theme backyard, where the natives were definitely restless, because of her. Emily was the reason he was there, and he could not just walk away.

He needed to know what had happened that night. He had never done anything so impulsive before. What was there about Emily that inspired instantaneous passion?

He wasn't a virgin by any means, but he also wasn't some superstud who went around proving he was a man by bedding every woman he met. The women who had traveled in and out of his life were mature, intelligent individuals, all of whom he respected. There hadn't been that many, and no broken hearts had been left in his wake. Except maybe for Georgia De Witt. He was almost positive that her heart hadn't been broken when he ended their engagement, but it should have been.

He had met Georgia years ago. They traveled in the same social circle and their paths had crossed many times. Over a year earlier she had needed an escort to some event and he had graciously agreed to accompany her. From that night on, they started seeing each other exclusively. They shared the same love of music, knew the same people, and enjoyed each other's company. Georgia was beautiful, gracious, intelligent, and totally undemanding. She had all the qualities of a perfect wife, so he had asked her to marry him and, surprisingly, she had accepted his proposal. Georgia had then thrown herself into the wedding preparations with the single-minded determination of a woman bent on achieving the social event of the year. When he had first started having doubts about marrying her, he had chalked it up to cold feet. When he had questioned himself about his lack of physical desire for his bride-to-be, he had reassured himself that he was being a gentleman. Georgia hadn't sent him any "burning passion" messages herself, but he had been positive their physical union on their wedding night would be quite satisfying.

He didn't consider himself a man of gut-wrenching passion. The kind of passion that inspired acts of heroism, movies, love songs, or poets just wasn't in him. He'd leave that kind of emotion to the Robin Hoods, Michael Boltons, and Lord Byrons of the world.

Or so he had thought, until he met Emily.

Something about Amelia Carmela Beaufont Pierce consumed him, body and soul. He wasn't leaving her home until he discovered what it was that made her so different from every other woman he knew.

He leaned against the picnic table and watched Emily as she received a sloppy, gooey kiss from the toddler in her arms. He shuddered at what that kiss might have left behind, but he had to admit, Christopher had very good taste in women. Emily didn't seem to mind the kiss, if her smile was any indication. She said something to the boy, who laughed in response. The love they shared was obvious.

Emily was a wonderful mother, he mused, then frowned as she lowered Christopher to the ground. The little boy ran toward a clump of bushes and squeezed in between two of them, immediately swallowed up by the shrubbery. Adam didn't want to associate Emily with being a mother. He didn't want to think about children, birthday parties, and toddler-eating shrubs. He wanted to concentrate on the woman herself and the way she had felt in his arms. He wanted to turn the clock back eight weeks, to when they had made love. He wanted to turn the clock forward, until he once again held her in his arms.

He shook his head and forced back the desire that had been building since he had stood on the porch and seen her for the first time in weeks. His physical response had been immediate and powerful, and he had been shocked once again at its intensity.

He squinted against the bright afternoon sunlight as Emily greeted a woman, obviously there to collect her child. Thankfully, the party was beginning to break up. Maybe if the noise level went from Super Bowl–stadium volume to something more humane, like a jackhammer pounding concrete, he could begin to think again. Another mother came from the side of the house, and a little girl ran toward her.

Adam discounted the other women and studied

Emily. She looked the way she had in the snapshot the detective had given him. Her hair was pulled up and back into a ponytail and held with a length of yellow ribbon. Navy blue shorts and a sleeveless yellow and white gingham blouse were both modest and cool. Her bare arms and legs were lightly tanned, and white sandals graced her feet. Toenails painted a soft pink peeked out from under the white leather. It was one of the things he remembered from that night. Her toenails had been painted pink, but not her fingernails.

Though she was attractive, her individual features weren't extraordinary. Her mouth was on the generous side and her nose was neither fat nor long. Her cheekbones were high and the curve of her chin hinted at a stubbornness he hadn't seen. It had been her eyes that had first captured and held his attention. She had soft green eyes surrounded by thick dark lashes that makeup hadn't created. Her eyes reminded him of the beginning of spring, before the rain and the sun sharpened the color of the leaves and the grass. He had always loved the approach of spring.

He had met more beautiful women, but none had affected him like Emily. Her voice was sweet and low and had been totally irresistible when she had begged him not to stop. Her fingers had been gentle, yet he had felt their strength as they had roamed his body. He even remembered the way her soft eyes had darkened to emerald fire as he'd slowly entered her, and the little purr that had escaped her throat when she had . . .

"Well, hello there, stranger." A voluptuous blonde blinked mascara-coated lashes at him and held out a hand. "I'm Mitzi Craig." She nodded in the direction of the house next door. "I live two doors down, and you must be new in the neighborhood."

Adam stared at her hand and the two-inch-long blood-red nails. He wondered if she had her claws registered with the police. "Adam Young."

Her smile grew flirtatious as she glanced around the yard. "Which one of these little darlings is yours?"

He had the distinct impression he was being sized up, and by the gleaming sparkle in Mitzi's brown eyes, he hadn't been lacking in any major departments. "None." He glanced over at Emily. She must have sensed his distress because she turned away from the woman she was talking to and looked at him. A slight smile pulled at her beautiful mouth when she noticed Mitzi by his side. He breathed a sigh of relief as she excused herself and headed in his direction.

"None?" Mitzi took a step closer and ran a long fingernail up his forearm.

He took a step closer to Emily as she joined them. "I'm a *friend* of Emily's," he said.

"Really, Emily," Mitzi purred. "I didn't realize you had such interesting *friends*." She eyed Adam once again. "Can I borrow him occasionally?"

Emily chuckled. "He's not a cup of sugar, Mitzi."

"But he looks awfully sweet."

Emily refused to glance at him. It was a good thing, he thought, because he was silently laughing at the exchange. He had a feeling Mitzi and Emily were more than good neighbors. They were friends, and Emily looked like she was used to Mitzi's outrageousness.

"Thanks for letting Shane come, Mitzi." Emily glanced over to where Shane was standing by the porch waiting for his mother. "I see he found his grab bag and is ready to leave."

Mitzi glanced at her son, then back to the man in front of her. "Oh, pooh, Emily, you're no fun." One long red nail tapped a button on Adam's shirt. "Any time you want to borrow a cup of sugar, sweet thing, you just stop on by and don't listen to a word Emily tells you about me." Her smile turned wicked. "My bite is definitely worse than my bark."

Adam grinned as Mitzi sashayed her way around the side of the house. He turned to Emily and said, "You have some very *friendly* neighbors."

"Don't flatter yourself. Mitzi's always lending out her sugar." She glanced at a man who had just walked into the backyard. "Excuse me, but Melissa's father is here."

Adam didn't like the friendly greeting Melissa's father gave Emily. He watched as a girl ran into the man's arms. Father and daughter exchanged a few more words with Emily, then left. That was more like the friendly suburban neighbors he had been expecting. He hadn't been prepared for Mitzi's blatant flirting or the way Emily had accepted it.

He watched as Emily and Jordon continued saying their good-byes to the party guests. Jordon kept glancing in his direction to see if he was still there, and he received quite a few stares from the parents. He sensed that Emily didn't usually have men about. He liked that notion, but not the curious stares.

As for Emily, she didn't turn around again.

THREE

Emily stood on the porch and watched as the last little smudged-faced, sticky-fingered party guest was driven away. Sighing wearily, she brushed back a few damp curls of hair that had escaped her ponytail. She was exhausted. She wanted nothing more than to sit in the shade of the porch in one of her grandmother's old rattan chairs, sip an iced tea, and watch the butterflies dance from flower to flower. It was a pleasant thought, but one that didn't have a snowball's chance in hell of coming true.

She had a million things to do. She had to wipe the first couple of layers of dirt off Christopher and put him down for his nap. Sam needed to be changed back into her usual shorts and top, and the once clean and pressed party dress would have to be tossed into the tub in the laundry room to soak if she was ever going to get it clean. The backyard needed to be straightened. She had to return the Humpheys' picnic table that she had borrowed. The kitchen was a disaster, and she still hadn't gotten the nerve to look in the downstairs bathroom that the party guests had been using for the past three hours.

The list was endless, but before she tackled the most pressing issues, she had one very important thing to do. She had to get rid of Adam Young.

The man was driving her crazy. She couldn't think when he was nearby. For the past hour she had been functioning on pure nervous energy. She had felt his every glance, and there had been many. What did he want with her? Why had he gone through all that trouble to locate her? Was he expecting to pick up where they had left off?

Emily cringed. They had left off sharing a shattering climax that had rendered her dazed, exhausted, and totally satisfied. Two hours later she had awakened to the sound of the shower running and pure horror had set in. What had she done? In a blind panic she had dressed and run from the hotel room. She hadn't stopped running until she was parked in her driveway staring at her house and the rising sun and wondering what in the world she was going to tell her sister, who was babysitting the kids. She most definitely did not want to pick up where they had left off.

What she wanted was Adam Young gone. Out of her life. Every time she looked at the man she felt mortified. She had to have been temporarily insane that night. There was no other explanation for what she had done. What they had done! Maybe it was the stress of raising three children on her own for the past two years that had made her finally crack. Or the fact that she had been so young when she had lost her husband, and she had been extremely lonely for a little male attention ever since. Or maybe her parents had been acid-dropping hippies in the sixties and she had experienced a flashback to free love. Impossible. She hadn't uttered the word "groovy" once that she could remember. That woman in the hotel room hadn't been her. It couldn't have been her. She hadn't even known it was possible to do half the stuff they had done!

Emily flushed as the memories poured over her and ignited an ache deep within her body. Her mind might rebel against the memories, but her body remembered his every touch. She didn't know what it was about Adam that inspired such a lustful response in her, but one thing was for certain. She had to get rid of him before she did something incredibly stupid, like repeat that night they shared two months ago.

She walked along the porch on the side of the house, and when she reached the backyard, she stared in amazement. She had only been out front for ten minutes, yet the changes in the yard were astounding. All the trash and toys had been picked up, her picnic table was spotless, even the grill and trash can were back in their proper places. The gate leading to the Humpheys' backyard was open, and she watched in wonder as Adam, Jordon, Sam, Christopher, and Wellington trooped back into her yard. They obviously had just returned the table she had borrowed. Adam looked like the Pied Piper leading the children and their dog through the gate.

She would have smiled if it wasn't scaring her so much. Jordon had that look on his face that clearly stated he had just found a new hero. Superman was about to be pushed to the end of the line. Samantha and Christopher both looked a little dazed by having a man help around the house. As for Wellington, who could tell what the dog was thinking with all that hair hanging in his face? The only thing she could see was his shiny black nose, and that didn't tell her anything.

"Hey, Mom, you should have seen it!" Jordon yelled the instant he spotted his mother.

"Seen what?" She stepped off the porch and crossed the yard to the group. The three dozen or so balloons she and Charmaine had tied to bushes and trees were still up, giving the backyard a festive look. The kids would enjoy playing in the brightly decorated yard for the next day or so, until the balloons started to lose their air.

"Mr. Young picked up the Humpheys' picnic table all by himself."

Yep, Emily thought. Superman had just landed on the top of the heap of discarded superheros. Adam was clearly king of the mountain. The round wooden picnic table wasn't exactly heavy, but it was awkward. A person needed the arm span of an eagle to reach from side to side. She glanced at the white polo shirt covering Adam's chest and shoulders. He obviously had that arm span. She had firsthand knowledge of the breadth of his shoulders and the muscles that rippled beneath his skin. Those muscles had trembled at her touch.

She felt heat flood her cheeks and pulled her gaze away from Adam's chest. The man was a threat to her sanity!

"That was very thoughtful of Mr. Young to return the table for us," she said to Jordan.

She glanced at Adam again, but kept her gaze focused on his chin. There was no way she could meet his eyes. "Thank you, Adam."

"No problem. The kids all helped by carrying the benches and showing me where it went."

He had a marvelous jaw, she mused. It was square and gave the appearance of both strength and refinement. A light shadow of beard blanketed his chin. She remembered the slight abrasion of the fine whiskers against her skin. When she had taken a shower after she'd gotten home that morning, his brand had been on her breasts, her stomach, and her thighs. She had been mortified by the red marks, but when they had faded away she had felt a sense of loss. The conflicting emotions had both confused and angered her.

She again jerked her gaze away from Adam and managed to smile at her children. "That was very helpful of you. Thank you." She glanced around the yard. "Did you also help clean up out here?"

"Mr. Young took care of the trash and stuff," Jordan said. "We did the toys and put all the food junk in the kitchen." The boy took a step closer to Adam and smiled.

Emily frowned. She usually had to resort to bribes,

threats, and a stern voice to get the children to coop-
erate so fully. She didn't like this at all. Jordon was
giving her the same look as he had when Aunt
Charmaine had surprised them both by giving him a
pet iguana for his fifth birthday. The pleading in his
brown eyes clearly said, "Please, Mom, please. Can we
please keep him?" It was one thing to have a twenty-
inch iguana named Elvis who periodically escaped his
cage and roamed the house. It would be something
else entirely to have a six-foot hunk named Adam
roaming the halls at night.

She needed to get Adam away from there, and the
sooner the better. "Jordon, please thank Mr. Young
for helping with your party. I'm sure he has somewhere else to go now, and we've imposed enough on
his time as it is."

"But, Mom . . ." Jordon began.

"Pooh," said Christopher.

Samantha disappeared behind the lilac bushes.
Adam just stood there watching her. He obviously
knew what she was doing, and he didn't look too
pleased with the idea of getting the bum's rush toward
the door.

Christopher toddled over to her and tugged on her
shorts. "Pooh," he demanded again, more urgently
this time.

Emily swept her sleepy son up into her arms.
When Christopher was tired and wanted his nap, he
always asked for his favorite bear, Winnie-the-Pooh.
She wasn't going to get a minute's peace from the boy
until he was tucked into his bed with Pooh and his

favorite, ratty-edged blanket. She cradled her youngest child closer.

"Jordon, please don't start. Your brother is tired and I need to get him settled down. Please thank Mr. Young for all his help."

Jordon kicked at one of the loose slates of the walkway and refused to look up. "Thanks, Mr. Young," he mumbled.

"You're welcome, Jordon. Why don't you call me Adam? All my friends do."

Jordon's head snapped up. "Really?"

"Sure, why not? Mr. Young is what everyone calls my father." He smiled at the boy before looking at Emily. "Why don't you put Christopher down for his nap? I'll keep an eye on these two for you."

"I really don't . . ."

"Please, Mom!" begged Jordon.

She'd seen it coming and still she wasn't prepared for the guilt that tugged at her heart. Jordon looked ready to cry, and all because she didn't want to face Adam alone. She was a coward. What kind of example was she to her children? Sighing, she hugged Christopher closer. "All right, Jordon. Adam can keep an eye on you and Sam for a minute. I'll be right back." She didn't have the nerve to look at Adam, so she turned and fled into the house.

Adam watched her go with a sense of relief. He knew she wanted to toss his butt off the property, and she would have, too, if it hadn't been for Jordon. The kid had a way with his mom. He guessed all kids could get one over on their moms, especially if the mom was as softhearted as Emily.

He had managed to get everything he ever wanted from his own mother, and he couldn't rightly say she was softhearted, but she did possess a good heart. Although Celeste Young had had more important things to do than to tuck him in for naps and throw noisy birthday parties, he'd had nannies, and then housekeepers, to tuck him in and see that he had everything he needed. Up until a few years ago his mother had been one of the country's top cancer research scientists. She had dedicated her life to stopping that horrible disease. At seventy-six she was now retired, but no one would know it by the schedule she kept. His father was seventy-seven and spent his days on the golf course. When winter approached, they packed their bags and their golf clubs and headed on down to sunny Florida, where they owned a condo overlooking the eighteenth hole.

Emily and her family were as different from his as public schools were from private schools. There was nothing wrong with public schools; they were just a world apart from the schools he'd attended.

He looked at his watch and sighed. By now he had hoped to have a private talk with Emily and dinner plans in the works. But then, he mused, nothing about this day was going as planned. So far he hadn't managed more than half a dozen sentences with her, and none of them needed privacy to be said. Maybe he could get a chance now, since Christopher was being put down for his nap. Surely Samantha and Jordon were old enough to play in the backyard without Emily watching over their every move.

"Hey, Adam, do you want to see what I got for my birthday?" Jordon grabbed his hand and started to pull him toward the house.

Emily was in the house, so Adam didn't resist until he remembered Sam was playing behind the bushes. "What about Sam?"

"She's okay. Mom lets her play in the yard all the time."

Adam glanced at the two overgrown lilac bushes. There wasn't a sign of the little girl or her doll. "Sam?"

"Yeah?" came floating back from between the leaves.

"I'm going inside with Jordon for a minute. Are you going to be all right out here by yourself?"

"Sure, Holly's with me."

Adam glanced at Jordon and whispered, "Who's Holly?"

Jordon whispered back, "Her doll."

Adam guessed that made sense. Mommies named their babies, so little girls had to name their dolls. "Okay, Sam. We'll be in the house if you need us."

As he followed Jordon in through the patio doors, he wasn't sure if he wanted to see the interior of the house. The exterior made him nauseous. The interior just might break his heart. He stepped into the large, airy kitchen and breathed a sigh of relief. While featuring all the modern conveniences, the room had kept its old-fashioned charm. Walls were painted a cheery yellow. The floor was the new resilient floor-ing, but it resembled the black-and-white-checkered pattern from the past. The wooden cabinets were painted white and boasted mullioned glass doors and shiny brass pulls. Assorted herbs were growing in bril-liantly colored pots on the windowsill.

If you disregarded the party clutter overflowing the counters and the massive pile of birthday presents on the kitchen table, it was a wonderful, welcoming room. It was the kind of room where you wouldn't mind having your first cup of coffee while reading the morning paper. His heart wasn't in danger of shatter-ing at how Emily had decorated the interior. If the kitchen was any indication, the rest of the house should be miraculous.

"See," Jordon said, "this is what Matt got me." He held up a plastic figurine of a horrible half-human, half-lion creature. "And this"—he picked up another figurine, this one resembling a wolf more than a man—"is from Shane."

Adam stood there and nodded his head as Jordon displayed one item after another. Jordon had received three baseball caps, two T-shirts, four trucks, one race car model, and an entire collection of mutant men and all the various equipment and vehicles needed to save or destroy the world. Which, Adam wasn't sure. Jor-don seemed immensely pleased with his haul. "That's a lot of presents, Jordon."

"Yeah, but you haven't seen the best one." Jordon grabbed his hand and tugged him into what should have been the formal dining room. Someone had been sadistic enough to cover the plaster walls with rooster print wallpaper. Hundreds of garish three-inch-high roosters glared at him from every direction. If that wasn't bad enough, the person had had the audacity to paint the trim of the entire room glossy red. He would have bet everything in his wallet that underneath that awful paint was hand-carved mahogany. Where an elegant chandelier should have been hanging was a black iron monstrosity that appeared to have miniature weather vanes in between the lightbulbs. A mud-colored rug covered the floor. In the middle of the floor stood a brand-new red bicycle, which Jordon had climbed onto.

"Your mom bought you a bike?" Adam guessed.

"No. Aunt Charmaine bought me the bike. She always buys us cool stuff for our birthdays and Christmas." Jordon nodded to a pile of boxes with shirts, shorts, jeans, and a pair of sneakers overflowing them. In a disgusted tone he said, "My mom always buys us clothes."

"That's because you would look awfully funny playing outside naked as the day you were born, Jordon Matthew Pierce."

Adam turned toward Emily, who had silently joined them. She stood in the doorway frowning at her son. She didn't look too pleased with her son's assessment of her gifts to him. He couldn't blame her, yet he could also sympathize with Jordon. To a seven-year-old, a bike would seem like a better present than a bunch of clothes. In an instinctive move he would have to think about later, Adam stepped closer to the boy and smiled at Emily. He didn't want Jordon to get into trouble with his mother, especially over something that he had said to him. "Jordon was just showing me what he got for his birthday. It looks like he made out real well."

Jordon got off his new bike. "Sorry, Mom. I really like the clothes, and the sneakers are cool. Shane has a pair just like them."

Emily's frown faded. "I know you would have rather I'd gotten you something 'cool' like the bike, honey. But you are the one who agreed to the deal."

"I know." He grinned at his mother. "The party was cool, Mom. Everyone said so." He raced across the room and threw himself into her arms. "Thanks, Mom." He kissed her cheek. "Can we finish the cake for dessert?"

Emily chuckled and returned the kiss with one of her own. "You just finished eating and already you're talking about dessert." She shook her head. "Why don't you go on out back and play with Sam for a while. We'll discuss dessert later."

Jordon was halfway through the doorway when he remembered Adam. He stopped and glanced at the man he considered his very own birthday wish. "Are you staying?"

Adam wasn't sure. It depended on Emily, and the way she had been reacting to his arrival, his money wasn't on staying. "I'll say good-bye before I leave," he told Jordon.

His response seemed to satisfy the boy, who said,

"Cool," and dashed through the kitchen and out the patio doors.

The screen door slid shut with a loud whooshing sound, and somewhere in the yard Wellington barked. Adam knew Emily was about to ask him to leave, but he hadn't the faintest idea how he would respond to her request. He couldn't very well tell her no. After all, this was her home. But he didn't want to leave, at least not yet. Somehow he knew if he mentioned that night they'd shared, she would push him away and out of her life. So he asked her the first innocuous question that came to him. "What deal were you and Jordon talking about?"

She glanced at the pile of boxes and clothes that had been regulated to the corner of the room. "Jordon had a choice, either a small party with his grandparents and aunt, clothes, and some *cool* toy, or a big party with all his friends being invited and the usual clothes from Mom. He picked the big party."

"Now I understand. You weren't mad with Jordon for grousing about the clothes, you were upset about him not owning up to the deal."

"He's only seven, but he has to learn to live with the decisions he makes."

"That's a hard lesson to learn sometimes." He wasn't referring to anything in particular, but by the blush that swept up her cheeks, he knew she was thinking about the decision she had made two months ago: the decision to step into a hotel room with him and spend the night. He still wanted to avoid discussing that night, though.

"I think—"

He cut her off before she could get another word out of her mouth. "Please tell me you didn't decorate this room."

She looked appalled as she glanced around the room. "You think I would do this to my grandmother's dining room?"

"Your grandmother did this?" He was the one who sounded appalled now. Some sweet old lady had done this to the house? Why hadn't Emily placed her in a nice nursing home when she lost her mind, instead of allowing her to destroy such a charming house?

"My grandmother is probably rolling over in her grave at what those *tenants* did to her house."

"Tenants?" He was extremely thankful that neither Emily nor any of her family had ruined the house. But why had there been tenants living there in the first place?

"It's a long story," she said, obviously guessing his silent question. She frowned once more at the barnyard wallpaper and walked back into the kitchen. She continued to frown at the clutter on the counters, but started to put it away.

"I love long stories," Adam said. He hadn't the foggiest notion if that was true, but considering the story would be coming from Emily, he was definitely interested in hearing it. He handed her a dirty plate as she opened the dishwasher.

She took the plate and placed it inside the dishwasher, then shrugged and started the story. "When my grandmother died seven years ago, she left me the house and my sister Charmaine got a nice-sized nest egg to put down on a house of her own."

"Why did she leave you the house and not the nest egg?"

"She knew how much I loved this house. Charmaine's taste runs toward the more modern end of the scale. When she was little, she tried to talk our grandmom into digging up the gardens out back and putting in an in-ground pool." Emily smiled at the memory as she placed the ketchup and mustard in the refrigerator.

He watched her mouth curve upward and felt its pull deep within his gut. "So why did you rent it out instead of living in it?"

"I was married, pregnant with Jordon, and living in Philadelphia at the time. My husband had just left a major advertising agency to start his own. Lititz was too far for a daily commute, and we simply couldn't afford the upkeep of two homes. I couldn't bear to part with it, so Ray suggested we rent it out and use the rent for taxes and any repairs that might be required, then take any profit to start a college fund for our unborn child." She tossed away some empty cups and wrapped a twist tie around the open end of the pretzel bag. "It seemed like a good idea at the time."

"Didn't you check on the house periodically?"

"The couple who rented it seemed nice. They paid the rent on time and never complained. They'd been here about a year when they called and asked my husband's permission to paint the place, and he said yes.

He looked at it as one less thing for us to worry about."

"Weren't you curious as to what they were doing?" He couldn't imagine professing to love a house and then not caring what tenants were doing to it. Something wasn't right.

"Charmaine doesn't live too far away and she occasionally drove down the street. She told me I really didn't want to know what was happening to the house and I agreed. There wasn't a whole lot I could have done about it after the fact."

Adam studied her. Her story had holes big enough to drive a truck through. He was more interested in what she wasn't saying than what she was. He glanced around the sunny kitchen and asked, "How long have you been living here?"

"Almost a year."

He held out the empty bowl the potato chips had been in. When she grasped the bowl, he tightened his grip. He waited until she met his gaze before asking, "Since your husband died?"

"It took me almost a year to sell the business and the house we had been living in." She took the bowl as he released it, and placed it in the dishwasher. "I also had to give the tenants four months' notice."

Her husband had died over two years ago, he thought. Christopher would have been only a baby, Sam would have been three, and Jordon probably hadn't even been in school yet. Lord, how had she managed everything? Three small children, a business and a house to dispose of, and the house she had loved all her life turned into a hideous blue monstrosity. The fact that she had managed, and by the looks of things, managed quite nicely, spoke a lot about Emily and her character.

The women he knew never would have survived. The disposing of the business and house wouldn't have posed a problem. They would have called their lawyers and accountants to handle the transactions. Moving into this house on its nice tree-lined street wouldn't have been an issue, although none of the women he had dated over the years would have actually lived there without calling in a team of decorators first. Except maybe for his former fiancée, Georgia. She had been surprising him lately, leaving him to believe he had never really known the woman behind the stunning face and perfect grace. But the part he knew would break every woman was the children. The mere thought of having three children would have had every woman of his acquaintance screaming in terror. To be left alone in life to raise three children would have driven them all over the edge.

He noticed the way Emily's soft green eyes continued to avoid his gaze. In the sunny light of the kitchen he could detect golden highlights throughout her hair. In the dimly lit hotel lounge and the room they had shared, he hadn't seen the golden strands or the four freckles that dotted her nose. The seductive curve of her lower lip he knew intimately both by touch and taste. Emily had tasted like sweet fire, and he hadn't gotten enough of her. He didn't think he would ever get enough of her, and that scared him.

What would he do if this flame of desire he felt for her didn't burn itself out? He had hoped by dropping in unannounced that he would find Emily doing something that would show him how wrong she was for him. Walking into a birthday party with a yard full of kids should have done the trick. He should have been long gone by now, so why wasn't he?

He watched as she turned away from him and put the remaining rolls into a bread box. His gaze immediately dropped to her backside and her long tanned legs. Her navy shorts weren't particularly tight or revealing. They weren't even very short. But they had to be the sexiest pair of shorts ever to caress a woman's bottom. Heat ignited low in his belly and the blood started to rush through his veins. He wanted her. He wanted her now. With two kids playing in the backyard and one upstairs napping, he still wanted to bury himself so deep within her that the pain from the last two months would fade away. For sixty-two days and nights he had lived in fear of not being able to find her again. Now that he had, all he could think about was hauling her off to the nearest bed.

He wouldn't blame her for throwing his sorry butt off her property. He deserved to be tossed out for having lecherous thoughts about her body while her children were running in and out of the house. He should be ashamed of himself, but he wasn't. He wanted her too much to be ashamed.

She turned around and gave him a questioning look. She seemed nervous, as if she knew exactly what he was thinking. She tried to read his eyes, but that seemed only to upset her more. He prayed his thoughts weren't readable.

He needed to say something to get his mind away from the direction it had taken. He opened his mouth and said the first thing he thought of that didn't pertain to her body, sex, or the way she tasted. "So, your son wants a dad for his birthday."

FOUR

The dishrag Emily had picked up to wipe the counters fell to the floor with a light splat. Her ears had to be deceiving her. She couldn't possibly have heard Adam right. "Excuse me, what did you say?"

"I was wondering why Jordon had wasted a good birthday wish on a dad. You seem to be doing a wonderful job raising him without one."

"Thank you." *I guess*, she added silently. She had to wonder if Adam was complimenting her on her child-rearing abilities, or if he wanted to make sure she knew he didn't see the need for him to be stepping into a daddy role. Which was fine by her. She wasn't looking for, nor did she want, a man to fill her late husband's shoes. Ray's shoes hadn't been that big, in fact they'd been practically nonexistent where the children were concerned. She had been raising the children without him while he was alive, and she didn't see any need to change that now that he was gone.

"Jordon made that wish because his friend Shane has been bragging about getting a new stepfather and all the wonderful things he's going to do with him." She bent down and picked up the dishrag and rinsed it out again in the soapy water in the sink. Shrugging, she added, "By tomorrow Jordon will be wishing for something else."

She kept her back toward Adam as she wiped the counters clean. She didn't want him to see her doubts. Jordon had never before expressed a desire to have a dad, at least not so openly. He had questioned his father's death, asking why *his* daddy had to go to heaven. But he had never mentioned a desire to replace him. Was it just a phase he was going through, brought on by Shane's remarks, or was there something more serious behind his out-of-the-blue birthday wish?

"What do seven-year-old boys wish for besides new bikes and mutant men?" Adam asked.

She smiled as she tossed the dishrag back into the sink. That was an easy one to answer. "Last week he wanted a pool in the backyard so he wouldn't have to wait until I had the time to take him and his brother and sister to the local pool. The week before that he had his eye on a pair of in-line skates. The week before that I think it was a skateboard. Then there was the trampoline, the radio-control car, the—"

Adam chuckled and held up his hands. "I get the picture." He glanced at the pile of toys sitting on the kitchen table. "Wouldn't it be easier just to move into a toy store?"

"Easier for whom, me or the kids?" She shook her

head at the absurdity of his statement. Who ever heard of just moving into a toy store and giving kids whatever they wanted? With surprising clarity she realized something. "You don't know much about children, do you?"

He gave her a wicked grin. "I know how they are made, and if my memory of health class is correct, they usually take about nine months to grow."

"That's it?" She couldn't believe that a man who appeared to have reached his mid-thirties knew so little about something as important as children. What had he been doing, living in a cave? He'd be a perfect candidate for Mitzi's "The Men I Will Marry" list. "Don't you have any nieces and nephews?"

"Not a one. I'm an only child." He picked up one of the baseball caps Jordon had gotten, stared at it for a moment, then shrugged and placed it back on the table. "I was the result of what's termed a 'surprise pregnancy.' "

"As in a good surprise or an accidental surprise?"

"Definitely accidental." Adam chuckled and relieved any worries she might have about him being hurt by his parent's unplanned accident. "My mother was forty when she had me, and she probably knew less about babies and children than I do now."

"Oh." How could a woman know less about children? What kind of childhood had Adam had? She studied him as he prowled her kitchen, looking for what, she hadn't a clue. He appeared fascinated by Jordon's pile of presents and the herbs she had growing on the windowsill. "What does your mother do?"

she asked. Any woman who'd been surprised by a late-in-life pregnancy and knew nothing about babies wasn't your typical housewife of the fifties.

"My mother was the head of a cancer research team at Johns Hopkins University. She's now retired, but you wouldn't know it by the number of committees and organizations she's involved with."

"Good Lord! What does your father do?"

"He was the chief cardiologist at Johns Hopkins University Hospital. Now he spends his days either on the golf course perfecting his stroke or at the hospital attending board meetings."

She was almost afraid to ask the next question, but she had to know. "What exactly do you do?" To think of the things they had done together, and she hadn't the first clue as to what he did for a living. With parents like that, she didn't even want to think about what career path he might have chosen. Whatever it was, it surely didn't leave a lot of time for a wife and family. For if it did, wouldn't he have one by now?

"I'm an architect."

Architect? That didn't sound too bad. Nice, sane nine-to-five job. No fourteen-hour work days, no working weekends, and no social climbing. None of the qualities she had hated so much in Ray's career. "What do you design, homes or commercial buildings?"

"A little of both, but currently we're working on a community."

"A community? How do you design a community?" As far as she knew, a community was a certain area that just kind of evolved. She didn't realize that someone actually went out and designed them.

"Have you heard of Lavender Hall Estates?"

"The new plush *everything* being built about ten miles out of Lancaster?" Lavender Hall was an historic old mansion falling into disrepair. It was surrounded by acres and acres of corn and tobacco fields. Several months ago the Lancaster newspaper had done a big splashy article on how the mansion was going to be restored to its former glory and used as a reception area for the planned estate. If she had read the article right, there was going to be a country club, golf course, and riding stables. In the first phase of development, a hundred single-family homes and just as many town houses were going to be built. If the article could be believed, there was a waiting list to be on a waiting list just to talk to the developers. No one applied to buy one of the homes; you had to be invited.

"That's the place." Adam gave her a small smile. "My firm designed it."

"Your firm?" Scratch everything she had been thinking about him holding a nice, normal job. He had his own firm that designed homes she couldn't afford the foyer in.

"Young Architects and Design."

"You designed everything at Lavender Hall Estates?"

"My employees or I did, except for the golf course. We called in the pros to design the course and to give us input on the clubhouse. The main buildings have been designed so far. Each home will be a custom design, so we've only done about a dozen of those. For the price these people are paying, they want and should have perfection."

Perfection! She wondered what kind of people could afford to buy perfection and why they would want to. Glancing around her kitchen, she thought about all the time and effort she had put into remodeling the room to her expectations. All the joy that planning had given her and the delight and sense of accomplishment she had felt when it was finally done. Was it perfection? No, but it was home. "How many employees do you have?"

"Counting secretaries and all, twenty-two. But I'll be hiring two more designers within the month."

Lord, his company was four times bigger than Ray's had been. And Ray's had killed him. What was this man doing in her kitchen? She should have sent him packing an hour ago. The little voice inside her head that had been tormenting her with the "What if" game had gone suddenly silent. There would be no more "what if he's the one," "what if you invite him to dinner," "what if he invites you to dinner," or "what if he kisses you?" The voice had been silenced. "You must be very proud of both yourself and your employees to get such a . . . what do you call it, a client?"

"It took months of hard work and seven-days-a-week schedules to win the contract with the developers of Lavender Hall Estates. Nothing came easy and the whole firm is determined to make Lavender Hall the shining jewel of not only the county but the tri-state area. There's already talk of a similar community being proposed outside of Baltimore."

She could hear the pride in his voice and shuddered. The memories of Ray's bragging about winning an account or impressing such and such a client came rippling back. The only difference was, Adam seemed to be proud of his whole firm, while Ray had only boasted about how *he* had done this or how *he* had done that. But in the end it was basically the same. Both men lived and breathed their businesses.

She had to put an end to Adam's visit. She couldn't keep pretending to herself any longer. Adam was there for only one reason, and that was to pick up where they had left off. The sooner he found out she wasn't going to jump into his bed, the sooner he would be leaving.

She glanced out the screen door and spotted Jordon and Sam playing at the far end of the yard. Privacy was something that came rarely in this house, so she squared her shoulders, looked Adam straight in the eye, and said, "I won't sleep with you again."

Adam felt as if someone had changed the script on him and he was left floundering on center stage. How did they get from discussing his work to sleeping together? "I don't remember asking you to."

Emily folded her arms across her chest. "You will."

"How do you know I will?" Her defensive posture wasn't lost on him. For some reason she felt threatened and unsure. And for some reason the threat seemed to have materialized out of the discussion they were having about his work.

Emily seemed to be having a hard time meeting his gaze, as if she suddenly realized she might have misjudged him. He felt like a heel, because she hadn't. He definitely wanted to haul her gorgeous tush back into his bed, but he hadn't shown up on her doorstep simply because of the sex. Something else about Emily intrigued him, something that went far deeper than just a gorgeous body and a mouth made for sin. That something had been driving him out of his mind for the past two months. Now that he had seen Emily in her own domain, surrounded by screaming children, hairy dogs, and a hideous blue Victorian house, he was more than intrigued. He was totally fascinated.

She shifted her weight from foot to foot, but kept her gaze squarely on level with his chest. "That's why you are here, Adam."

"I won't lie to you, Emily. I definitely want you back in my bed, but that's not the reason I showed up today."

"Then why did you?" Heat had flooded her face with his blunt words.

"I came to ask you to dinner."

"Dinner?"

He almost smiled at her look of surprise. What did she think he was going to do, drag her to the nearest bed and ravish her? It wasn't a bad idea, but his parents had raised him to be a gentleman. First you fed your date, then you could ravish her. Well, that didn't quite apply. The night he'd met Emily, he had only bought her a glass of champagne, which she had never even touched. "You have something against dinner?"

"I . . ." She shot a quick glance out the screen door in the direction of the kids. "I don't date, Adam. I'm sorry if I gave you the wrong impression."

He wasn't sure if he should curse her stubbornness or laugh at the absurdity of it all. She was sorry if she gave him the wrong impression! The woman spent an entire night in his bed doing the most marvelous things to both his body and his mind and she was worried about giving him the wrong impression! The impression she had left him with was that he had finally found the element that had been missing from his life. Of course, when he had opened the bathroom door that morning, he had discovered she was also missing from his bed. He wasn't about to let her send him away because of a little embarrassment.

"What do you mean you don't date? The night we met, you told me your date had been called away on some emergency."

"It wasn't a real date."

"How do you have a fake date?"

Emily sighed and kept her gaze on the screen door and the children beyond. "It was a birthday present from my sister. She gave me two tickets to see the Philadelphia Orchestra perform at the Fulton Opera House. She also babysat and lined me up with an escort for the evening. John was nice enough to suggest dinner afterwards, but he was called away just as dessert was being served."

"What was the emergency?"

"There was a four-car pileup on Route 30. A seven-year-old had multiple compound fractures.

John's an orthopedic surgeon at Lancaster General. He specializes in pediatrics."

Adam gave a low whistle. Doctor John should apply for sainthood, both because of his career choice and because of his ability to walk out of a restaurant and leave Emily sitting there all alone. He would be indebted to the good doctor for life. "How many times has Doctor John called you since that night?"

"Three."

He was beginning to dislike Doctor John. "How many times has he asked you out?"

"Three."

"How many times did you say yes?"

"None."

"Now you know why I showed up in person instead of calling. It's too easy to say no over the phone."

She looked away from the door and straight at him. "I'm saying no in person, Adam."

He could see the determined tilt of her chin. Instead of arguing with her, he asked again, "Why don't you date? It can't be from the lack of offers. You're a beautiful, intelligent woman. You can't mean to tell me that fix-up with Doctor John was your first date since your husband passed away?"

"Fine, I won't tell you, then."

Adam felt his heart jump into his throat. She was telling the truth. She hadn't been out with anyone since her husband was buried two years ago. That meant he was the first man since . . . Lord, have mercy. If he had known that, he would have . . .

Would have what? Been gentler? Slower? He prayed he would have been both, but deep down inside he doubted if things would have been any different. The heat that had erupted between them had been too intense to be contained by civil trappings. They had barely made it to the bed the first time they'd made love.

He could tell by the blush that stained her face that she knew what she was telling him. That he was the first man since her husband to touch her, to hold her, to make love to her. He could also tell that she wasn't ready to discuss that night. He wasn't too concerned about the past, though. He was more worried about the future. Their future.

"Are you still in love with your husband?" It made perfect sense to him. She was still in love with the guy two years after his death. What other reason could she have for not dating? Two years was more than a respectable mourning period.

"That's a highly personal question."

"A lot of what we did, Emily, was 'highly personal.' " He flinched as the color faded from her face. She was going to toss him right out the door, and he couldn't blame her. He never should have mentioned her late husband. And he definitely never should have thrown their night together in her face like that. Every ounce of refinement and decorum he possessed seemed to flee the moment he stepped within twenty yards of her.

Her gaze seemed riveted to the floor. "My feelings toward Ray have nothing to do with why I don't date."

The fact that she didn't directly answer his question didn't go unnoticed. He didn't push that issue; he was too damned thankful she hadn't told him to shove his questions where the sun didn't shine. But if her late husband wasn't the reason, what was? "What or who does?"

Her back stiffened and she raised her chin. "They have three names. Jordon, Samantha, and Christopher."

"Your kids?"

"Unless you know of some other Jordon, Samantha, and Christopher."

Now he was confused. Where did the kids fit into all of this? He knew she had children. Millions of single mothers throughout the world dated. Single fathers dated. Sometimes they even dated each other. "What does your having kids have to do with your not dating?"

Emily released a sigh that seemed to come from the depths of her soul. "I guess you have to have children to understand, Adam."

"Tell me, Emily. Make me understand."

This time her sigh sounded more like a groan, but she responded. "What did you want me to do with Jordon, Sam, and Christopher while we went out and had dinner? Call a sitter at four o'clock on a Saturday? I would have a better chance of space aliens landing in the front yard than locating a reliable sitter this time in the afternoon. Teenagers today have more important things to do than babysit. There are malls to hang out in, navels to pierce, and blue hair dye waiting to be tried. Every time I want to go out to dinner or a movie, I'm supposed to pay a stranger to watch my kids? I won't call my parents to sit with the kids while I go out and paint the town red. They both still work full-time, and besides, they're my kids, my responsibility, not theirs. I can't see me calling my former-in-laws so I can go out with some other man, can you?

"I won't even begin to get into the emotional upheaval my dating would cause the children. They could resent you or any other man for taking their mommy's time away from them. That should make for a real enjoyable relationship. Or worse. Suppose the kids really like the man I date and think he's the best thing since Big Bird and The Cartoon Network. What happens when the relationship ends? Not only does it affect two adults, but three innocent children get hurt as well."

Adam almost smiled. Obviously, Emily had stepped up on her soapbox and was letting him have it with both barrels. Most, hell, probably *all* of her points were valid, but he still didn't like her answer. What was she supposed to do, forget that she was a woman until the children were all grown up with lives of their own?

"It sounds like you've given the subject some serious thought," he said. Actually, it sounded to him like at one time she'd thought about dating, then had neatly and precisely listed all the reasons why she shouldn't. He was curious to know exactly when she'd first considered dating. Was it before or after she had met him?

"I . . ."

Her voice trailed off as Jordon and Sam rushed into the house as if the sky had started to fall. The sliding screen door opened with a bang. Before they could close it, Wellington bounced into the room with a resounding bark and as much grace as an elephant in a strawberry patch. The screen door slid shut with another loud bang.

"Hey, Mom," Jordon shouted as he headed for his presents and started to plow through them, "what's for dinner?"

"We just cleaned up from a late lunch." Emily's hand shot out and grabbed Samantha before she could sneak out of the room. "You, young lady, need to be cleaned up."

Adam tried to keep track of the commotion. His gaze bounced from Jordon, to Emily, to Sam's ruined dress, to Wellington attacking a water dish as if he had just crossed the Sahara, and then back to Emily. How could anyone follow the conversation, or was it conversations? Everyone was talking at once. Samantha was complaining about getting changed, Emily was muttering about the dress and how she would never get it cleaned, and Jordon wanted dinner. Wellington was still slurping away at the five-gallon bowl of water. Drops of water were flying everywhere.

"But, Mom," Jordon whined, "I didn't have time to eat. There were too many other things to do."

"I know for a fact that I handed you a hamburger not more than an hour ago. What happened to it?"

Emily pulled a twig and a couple of leaves from Sam's braid as she looked at her son.

"It fell on the ground and Wellington ate it." Jordon selected a Phillies baseball cap and jammed it on his head. "Can we order in pizza tonight?"

"Not tonight, Jordon." Emily grabbed a big yellow towel that had been hanging near Wellington and held it out with both hands. Adam watching in amazement as the dog shoved his head into the towel and rubbed it back and forth. The dog appeared to be drying its hairy face. Emily completed the job and secured the towel back on its hook. Wellington used his head to shove a chair out of his way and maneuvered his bulky body under the kitchen table. With what sounded like a yawn, the dog lay down and promptly fell asleep.

"But, Mom, it's my birthday."

"I know we usually have pizza on birthday nights, but since Aunt Charmaine or Grandpop and Grandmom aren't here, I don't see the need to test the pizza shop's promise to deliver in twenty minutes or the pizza is free."

"But we have company." Jordon looked at Adam and grinned. "Doesn't Adam count as company?"

Adam looked at Emily and smiled. Jordon once again was saving him from being tossed out. "I have a suggestion," he said. "Why don't you change Sam into something a little more dirt resistant? Jordon can put away his presents. And when Christopher wakes up from his nap, we can order in pizza and time them. My treat."

"Please, Mom," Jordon begged.

He could see Emily's indecision. She was probably running through her list of all the reasons she couldn't date. "Come on, Em," he teased, "it's only pizza, nothing more. I was so busy earlier that I didn't even get a hamburger." He hadn't been hungry then, and he wasn't really hungry now, but he wasn't about to pass up an opportunity to stick around for a little while longer.

Emily relented reluctantly. "I guess."

"Yea!" Jordon shouted. "Can we get extra cheese on it?"

"Since it's your birthday, you can get whatever you want on it," Adam said.

"Yea!" Sam yelled as she kicked off her dirty dress shoes. "Can I get fishies on mine?"

Adam shuddered. What five-year-old kid ate anchovies on her pizza?

"No, you may not have anchovies, Sam," Emily said. "I told you before, the fish aren't alive, so you can't add them to your aquarium." Emily glanced at Adam and shrugged. "She saw them on somebody's pizza once, and ever since she thinks it's like winning goldfish at the fair."

He could only nod his head as if he understood. Words had totally failed him. Maybe Emily was right after all; moms shouldn't date, especially men who knew absolutely nothing about children. He watched as Jordon scooped up a pile of toys and dashed out of the room. Wellington snored under the table and hit the leg of a chair with one of his paws. He seemed to be dreaming about something. Sam flashed him a smile that reminded him of Emily's. Funny things happened to his chest as the small girl hurried after Jordon. Two pairs of pounding footsteps racing up the stairs echoed throughout the kitchen.

Emily shrugged again, giving him a bewildered look that clearly showed she was questioning his sanity and her own. "Make yourself at home. I'll be right down." She headed out of the kitchen, leaving him alone with a snoring dog.

He stared at Wellington, at the damp yellow towel hanging by the water dish, and then out the screen door to where gaily colored balloons still decorated the bushes and trees. This was definitely not home. Home to him was a plush modern condo on the outskirts of Lancaster. He had designed the buildings and each unit himself about five years earlier. He had recently been toying with the idea of purchasing one of the two-acre lots available in Lavender Hall Estates and designing himself a house.

He could hear footsteps running around upstairs, directly above his head. He glanced up and stared at the ceiling. Jordon's voice was muffled and distant. Sam's shrill laughter was not. He cringed as somewhere a door banged shut. How was little Christopher sleeping through all the racket?

He wondered, not for the first time and, if his reaction to Emily was any indicator, not for the last time, what exactly he had gotten himself into.

FIVE

Emily watched the red glare from Adam's tail lights until they disappeared down the street and out of sight. He was gone. She should be relieved he had finally left. So why wasn't she? She turned her gaze to her children playing in the yard behind her. Jordon and Sam were busy trying to catch lightning bugs, which were just coming out at dusk. Christopher was still counting his rock collection on the porch. It was cute the way he only knew how to count up to three, then had to start all over again.

She had been positive Christopher's counting up to three twenty or thirty times in a row would have driven Adam to the breaking point, but he hadn't seemed to mind. He had tried a few times to get Christopher to say "four," but every time, her son would shake his head and go right back to "one."

The pizza had been delivered with two minutes to spare, and the meal had been surprisingly enjoyable.

Adam had seemed a little shell-shocked by the constant conversation, but he had held on admirably. The children hadn't batted an eye at having him join them for dinner. The excitement of the party had prevailed throughout dinner, with Jordon retelling everything he and every other party guest had done.

Adam had helped once again to clean up, then they had all gone out front to see Jordon try out his new bike. Sam had ridden up and down the sidewalk on her bike while Christopher had pedaled his tricycle closer to home. Adam and Emily had stood on the walk and watched the kids. It had felt so damn normal having him beside her that it had scared her to death. When she'd told the kids it was starting to get dark and to put the bikes away, Adam had said it was time for him to go.

She should have been relieved he was finally leaving. Yet at his words, a feeling of emptiness had opened in the pit of her stomach.

The kids had said their good-byes to Adam, then went to put away their bikes. She had politely walked Adam to his car and thanked him for helping with the party and for the pizza. She had been expecting another dinner invitation and had been prepared to refuse him again. None came. He had stood by the door of his expensive luxury car and stared at her for a full minute before saying he'd be in touch. Then he'd gotten into his car and driven away.

She had felt the heat of his gaze as they'd stood by his car, seen the hunger that burned in his eyes. He had wanted to kiss her. She knew it and he knew she knew it. But he hadn't. Something had stopped him.

It hadn't been her.

With his gaze scorching her mouth, she wouldn't have stopped him. She had wanted that kiss just as much as he had. And he had known it. So why hadn't he pulled her close and taken what she would have freely given?

Emily kept her gaze on her children as she walked up the path to the porch. She knew the reasons—Jordon, Samantha, and Christopher. They were her heart.

Emily stared at the book in her hands and wondered why she couldn't even bring herself to open it. It was the latest best-seller from her favorite mystery writer. The previous night, before her eyes had become too tired for her to keep on reading, she had narrowed the field of suspects down to three, and her money had been riding on the husband's mistress, who was also fooling around with the detective in charge of the case. Of course, that left the golf pro who used his international fame to smuggle dope to pay off a blackmailer, and the calm, meek zoologist. Nobody threw in an unimportant zoologist in the middle of a murder investigation without good reason.

Tonight, though, she had more important things on her mind than a good whodunit. *Adam was back in her life!* The hot, liquefying feeling in the pit of her stomach was once again melting its way down to her toes. It was the same weird sensation she had experienced when she had glanced across the crowded lobby of the hotel and spotted him two months ago. The memory was so clear in her mind, it could have happened last night instead of eight weeks ago. . . .

She had finished eating dessert all alone in the secluded, fern-draped dining room. Or to be accurate, she had just finished pushing pieces of the delicious chocolate mousse pie around her plate and feeling sorry for herself. Tonight was her thirty-second birthday and she had never felt so alone in her life. Her date, John, had been courteous and attentive until he had to leave to handle an emergency. She couldn't fault him for leaving. She faulted herself for expecting too much out of a simple evening out. What she had been expecting, she wasn't really sure herself. All she knew was that that afternoon she had blown out her birthday candles with the wish that tonight would be special. A special evening spent in the company of a handsome, charming man wasn't too much to wish for, was it? It had been so long since she'd felt special where a man was concerned. Tonight she had wanted to be a woman, not just a mother to her children.

She left the dining room and was crossing the lobby when she felt someone staring at her. She glanced to the right and encountered the intense gaze of a stranger. His looks went beyond handsome. Charmaine would have labeled him hunk material. Mitzi, her neighbor and friend, would have called him a bedtime snack.

Heat erupted like a volcanic explosion in her stomach and melted its way past her knees and down to her toes. She stumbled slightly and then he was there, directly in front of her, asking her to dance. Low, slow music was wrapping its way across the lobby and pulling her toward the lounge. She accepted his offer. What could one dance hurt?

By the second dance she was so hot, she was amazed that the dress she was wearing didn't erupt in flames. Adam was the perfect gentleman. His hands never strayed inappropriately and she had to give him credit for trying to start a conversation. She, however, was beyond forming coherent sentences. She vaguely remembered telling him her first name and something about her sister. Beyond that, she hadn't a clue. All she kept thinking was that birthday wishes did come true. Adam Young, stranger, gentleman, and gorgeous hunk, was holding her in his arms as if she were the most precious woman in the world and he wasn't about to let her go. She didn't want him to. She wanted to stay in his arms forever.

The third song was "Some Enchanted Evening," and as it drew to an end and the piano player announced it was time for his break, Adam asked her to stay. She knew what he was asking, and despite everything she had been taught and believed, she said yes. How could she refuse? This was her enchanted evening. Adam Young was her birthday wish.

He walked her to a small table, held her chair while she sat, and bought her a glass of champagne. She had four minutes to think about her decision while he stepped out of the lounge. She watched as one bubble after another floated to the top of her drink, but she didn't taste the lightly gold liquid. Alcohol wasn't going to be a factor in her decision. Heat, need, and the burning desire to feel this man's touch were enough to make her stay seated in the shadowy lounge.

When Adam returned, he simply held out his hand and

she went willingly. They didn't talk in the elevator on the ride up to the fourth floor, or when he opened the door with the plastic card key. There wasn't anything to say, or maybe there was too much to say. When the door locked behind them, he pulled her into his arms and claimed her mouth.

His kiss was neither gentle nor demanding. Adam Young kissed her as if he had done it a thousand times before. His hands pulled her closer and she knew there would be no turning back. Heat built and clothes were cast aside in a jumbled mess as they stumbled across the room to the bed. Adam's hands and mouth were everywhere, touching, caressing, and stroking. She returned his attention with a feverish frenzy of kisses and strokes of her fingertips.

He barely managed to put on protection before they tumbled to the bed and he dove into—

Brrring! The ringing of the phone shattered the erotic memory.

Emily dropped her book and grabbed the phone before it rang a second time. She didn't want the ringing to wake the kids. "Hello?" Her voice cracked with the aftershock of feverish memories. The clock on her nightstand showed her it wasn't quite eleven o'clock. Who would be calling at this time of night?

"Emily?"

She pulled the receiver away from her ear and stared at it. "Adam?" Talk about an embarrassing coincidence! Heat was still burning her body and her breasts felt heavy and swollen.

"Who else were you expecting a call from?"

"No one. I wasn't really expecting a call from you

either." Truth be told, she thought she would never hear from him again.

"I told you I'd be in touch."

She glanced again at the bedside clock. "That was only about two hours ago."

"I wanted to give you enough time to give the kids their baths and do whatever it is moms do with kids before they tuck them in for the night."

"Moms do all kinds of different things. It depends on the kids and the moms."

"What do you do?"

Emily took a deep breath and relaxed, settling herself more comfortably against the headboard of her bed. The peach-colored sheet and blanket were bunched at the bottom of the bed, where she had kicked them off during her daydream. A gentle breeze was rustling the curtains. She could hear the sound of crickets as they rubbed their legs together and serenaded the night.

No one had ever wanted to know how she tucked the kids in at night before. If Adam had been standing in front of her, she probably would have shrugged off his question. But he wasn't there, he was calling her from his home. The distance between them made her feel safe, while his deep voice filled her with a longing that could never be satisfied. Ray had never cared how the children were put to bed. Half the time he hadn't even been home.

"Jordon's at the age where he doesn't want me to do too much of anything. He likes to think he's independent enough to shower and get himself into bed.

But I think he likes it when I stop in to make sure he's all right and to kiss him good night.

"Sam has this routine where we have to tuck in her dolls and make sure they all receive a kiss before the lights go out. Christopher gets to choose a book. I sit in a rocking chair in his room, he climbs on my lap, and I read to him. He gets one book read and two kisses because that's how old he is."

Adam was quiet for a long time before he asked, "You're a very good mother, aren't you?"

She grinned. "I like to think so. But I really can't answer that yet. I've got years and years ahead of me. Someone once told me that once you become a mother, you will always be a mother. The job doesn't end when they leave for college, move out on their own, or start their own families. The job's a lifelong commitment."

"I think you're a wonderful mother, Emily."

It was probably the highest compliment anyone had ever given her, but she couldn't accept it. "How can you say that, Adam? You really don't know me at all."

"I would like to."

His voice was husky and sensual, sending shivers down her spine and goosebumps to her arms. Something about hearing his voice while lying in bed was combustible. It brought back the memories of that night in vivid detail. Memories of what his mouth had said and done to her. Magic memories. Hot memories. Memories that made her ache with need and burn with embarrassment. "I told you, Adam, I don't date."

"I'm not asking you for a date, Em."

Em. No one had ever called her just Em. Her grandmother had called her Amelia. Her parents and friends had shortened the formal and old-fashioned name to Emily. Even Ray had called her Emily. But Adam had called her Em that night. He had whispered it, groaned it, chanted it. *"Em, I want you." "Em, I need you." "Please, Em, now . . . I can't last much longer. . . . Come with me, Em. . . . That's it, Em. . . . I got you, Em. . . . Oh, Em, Em, Em . . ."*

"Em, are you still there?"

His voice snapped her out of the past. "I'm—" She had to clear her throat before continuing. "I'm sorry, Adam." She reached for the sheet and pulled it up to her chin. Despite the warmth of the June night, she suddenly felt a chill seep into her bones. She was cold and lonely, just like her bed. The sigh that escaped her sounded bleak even to her ears. "If you don't want a date, what do you want from me?" she asked. Why was he doing this to her? She wasn't really good at resisting temptation.

"I didn't say I didn't want to go out with you, Em. I just said I wasn't asking." He let a few seconds tick by before softly adding, "Yet."

Emily closed her eyes and prayed for strength. The man was relentless and she could feel herself weakening. It was the same feeling she got every time she walked into Lied's bakery and saw the tray of double fudge brownies. They were oh, so good but oh, so bad. "Adam, please."

"I just want to talk, Em. Nothing else."

Talk! She almost laughed. What else could they possibly do on a telephone? It wasn't his fault her mind was wandering down memory lane. "What do you want to talk about?"

He hesitated as if considering what to say or how to say it. After a moment he asked, "When are you going to get rid of those god-awful roosters in the dining room?"

She again relaxed against the headboard and smiled. He wanted to talk about the hideous wallpaper in the dining room. Of all the subjects that had raced through her mind, wallpaper hadn't been one of them. "As soon as I work up enough energy to start stripping the walls and woodwork, the barnyard will be gone."

"Mom!" Jordon shouted as he ran out of the living room and thundered down the hall toward the kitchen. "I can't find Elvis!"

Emily nearly peeled the top three layers of skin off the tip of her thumb with the potato peeler. "What do you mean, you can't find Elvis? Isn't he in his cage?" The last thing she needed was her son's iguana loose in the house. The last time the reptile escaped, it had taken them two days to find him, and then he hadn't been too pleased about leaving his new home behind the water heater in the basement.

"I took him out of his cage and brought him downstairs." Jordon dashed around the kitchen looking behind and under everything.

"Why did you do that?" Emily dropped the potato she had been peeling and quickly washed her hands.

"I wanted to show him to Adam when he came." Jordon hurried through the empty dining room and into the front parlor. "He didn't get a chance to meet him yesterday."

Emily followed her son and scanned each room as she went. Elvis was an expert at hide-and-seek. "Adam's not even here yet, Jordon. All he said was, he'd stop in after lunch." She wasn't even sure how that had happened.

Last night she hadn't hung up the phone until after midnight. They had talked for an hour about old houses, what this house had looked like when she was a little girl, and what her visions for its future included. Adam had been a wealth of information and had seemed to know exactly what she'd been talking about. He had mentioned having some great reference books and mail-order catalogs that might interest her. The next thing she'd known, he had mentioned stopping over to drop off the books, then he'd said good night. It had taken her a long time to fall asleep.

Maybe she shouldn't have told the kids Adam would be stopping by. They were going to be awfully disappointed if he didn't show up. She refused to dwell on how she'd feel. She didn't want to know.

Jordon dashed back out into the hall in his frantic search for the four-footed Elvis, who most definitely wasn't wearing blue suede shoes. She took the more logical approach. She knelt down in front of the couch and started to sing "Hound Dog." Elvis wasn't called

Elvis for nothing. The green lizard loved The King's songs. She bent over and peered under the couch. Nothing but two Barbies and a dusty rubber ball.

Emily stayed on her knees and scanned the surrounding floor as she headed for the chair. She found the missing piece from the Candy Land game and another ball, but no lizard. She crawled to the secretary that had been her grandmother's and that was sitting crosswise in one corner of the room. Last month Elvis had managed to wiggle his way behind the heavy piece of furniture and she had had to call her dad over to help move the thing. "Jordon," she yelled over her shoulder, "make sure all the doors are closed!" She didn't need to search every room of the house, and Elvis was an excellent climber. If he got outside, they might never catch him.

She heard a commotion out in the hall and figured Jordon had enlisted the help of his sister. She heard the front screen door close and yelled louder, "Don't go outside; we don't want him to escape!" She was lying on the floor trying to look behind the desk, softly singing "Love Me Tender," when she heard someone, probably Jordon or Sam, enter the room. "No signs of Elvis back here." She pushed herself to her knees and without turning around asked, "Any signs of him out there?"

"Last week I heard they spotted him in Iowa at the grand opening of a Wal-Mart." Adam's voice was laced with laughter. She spun around, and he held out a hand to help her to her feet.

"You're here." She fought the flush stealing up her

face. She had absolutely nothing to be embarrassed about. There was a perfectly good explanation why she was on her hands and knees searching for Elvis. If Adam ever got that stupid grin off his face, she just might tell him.

"Yes, I'm here and"—he nearly choked on his laughter—"Elvis is not."

Emily glanced one last time around the room. Not a lizard in sight. "You're right. Elvis isn't in here."

"Jordon let me in and then he went dashing off somewhere. He seemed to be looking for something."

"Really? I can't imagine what." She led Adam back out into the hall. There wasn't any place for Elvis to hide there. The settee was dainty and elegant. She noticed a stack of books and catalogs sitting on it. The hat rack combined with a large mirror was adorned with a few choice hats she had picked up at local flea markets. Only two houseplants, which couldn't survive the bright summer sun, remained in the hall. Elvis loved the hallway in the winter with its monstrous plants. It looked like a jungle to her when she brought the plants back in; to Elvis it probably resembled the entire rain forest of Brazil.

Samantha came hurrying down the stairs singing about a teddy bear. The way she was massacring the tune, only her mother would know it was an old Elvis tune. She spotted Adam standing with her mother. "You're here!"

Adam grinned at the little girl, then at Emily. "So I've been told."

Samantha skidded to a stop in front of them just as

Jordon came out of the small bathroom/laundry room shaking his head. Christopher was two steps behind him. Emily knew that look. Elvis was still on the loose. "Let's look in the living room," she said.

She turned to the only room on the first floor left to search. She had learned over the past three years how to systematically search for Elvis. Closest areas first. Elvis might be an excellent hider, but he thought slow on his feet. As long as you didn't give him too much of a head start, he was easy to find. He usually ran for the first cover he could find. From there he figured out his next move.

Adam followed the kids and Emily into the living room. He watched as they spread out and started to search the room. With a shrug he followed Emily's example and knelt in front of the couch as she knelt in front of the chair. He watched as she lifted the skirting and looked under. His hand was on the skirting of the couch when he glanced at her again. "What exactly are we looking for?"

"Elvis," she said.

"Elvis," Jordon said as he looked behind the toy box.

"Elvis," Samantha said as she looked behind the television.

Adam was about to ask what Elvis looked like, but he already knew what Elvis looked like. White sequined jumpsuit, black hair, sideburns. He chuckled at the picture forming in his mind. More than likely, Elvis was one of the two cats Emily had said they owned. Yesterday he hadn't had the opportunity to meet the felines. He bent, lifted the green plaid couch skirting, and froze in horror. A frightful hissing sound greeted his intrusion, and inhuman gold eyes stared at him. He jumped back a good foot and bumped into the coffee table. "Emily?"

Four heads had turned in his direction at the hissing sound. Emily's eyes were filled with laughter and her mouth was curved into a smug smile. "Yes, Adam?"

Adam knew the joke was on him. "Either Elvis is a lizard or the ugliest darn cat I've ever seen."

The kids started to laugh. Jordon knelt down, reached under the couch, and pulled. Elvis didn't look too happy about being found, but Jordon managed to haul him up onto the coffee table, avoiding his whipping tail. "He's not a cat, he's an iguana." Jordon scratched the top of Elvis's head. The tail stopped slashing back and forth, and the lizard hissed again, this time playfully.

Adam glanced between the kids and their interesting choice of pets. None of them seemed intimidated by the green reptile with a comb of scales running down the middle of its back. "Does he always roam the house?"

"No," Jordon said. "He stays up in my room in his cage. I brought him down so you could see him, and he got away from me." He gave his mother a small smile. "Sorry, Mom."

"You know you weren't supposed to take him out of the cage without asking me first," Emily said to her son, then shook her head at Elvis. "If you don't stop running off and hiding, I won't buy you any more Elvis tapes to listen to." She reached over and scratched its head, chuckling at its hiss. "Don't give me that look. You know you were bad."

Adam wasn't positive, but the damn thing appeared to be smiling.

"Jordon," continued Emily as she watched Sam and Christopher scratch Elvis's head, "you know Michelangelo and Leonardo don't appreciate Elvis cutting in on their territory."

Adam nervously glanced around the room as he got up off the floor and sat on the sofa. "Excuse me, Em, but who—I mean, what—are Michelangelo and Leonardo?" Any family that kept an iguana in the house couldn't be trusted to have common sense when it came to pets.

"They're our cats." She gave him a look that clearly said she knew what he was thinking. "Remember I mentioned them to you yesterday?"

"Right, but you didn't mention their names. Why did you name them after artists?" He was breathing a little easier. Cats, he could handle. Iguanas, he wasn't too sure about.

"I didn't." She picked up Christopher, who was becoming a little bit too rough with old green Elvis. "The kids named them after the Ninja Turtles."

"You named your cats after turtles?"

"Not just any turtles, superhero turtles." She placed Christopher on a chair, then handed him a red plastic fire truck that had been in the toy box. "They wanted to name them Daffy and Bugs, but I vetoed that suggestion. Leonardo and Michelangelo sound classier, don't you think?"

"Uh, sure." At this point he didn't know what to think. He still hadn't met the dynamic duo of the feline world, so he wanted to hold back judgment. The darling little kitties might turn out to be Siberian tigers.

Emily reached down and picked up Elvis. Adam noticed how she held the tail in one hand to prevent being whipped by the thing. "I'll go put The King back in his cage." She glanced at Jordon and Sam. "You two entertain our guest. I'll be right back."

She strolled from the room, cradling the lizard as if it were a baby. Adam could just hear her soft humming. She was humming "I'm So Lonesome I Could Cry" to an iguana.

"Hey, Adam, want to see my fishies?" Sam asked.

Lord, he had completely forgotten about Sam's aquarium. "Sure, honey. Give me a minute to recover from meeting Elvis first." He looked at Jordon and asked, "How many more animals do you have living here?"

Jordon had to think. "There's Wellington, Michelangelo, Leonardo, Elvis, Sam's fish, and Christopher has a bug house."

"A bug house?" What in the world was a bug house?

"Mom bought it for him." Jordon held up his hands and measured about eight inches of air. "It's about this big and it's made out of wood and screens. It even has a little door."

"What does he have in it?" Sounded harmless enough, but Jordon had just pulled a lizard as long as his arm out from underneath the couch.

"Last I looked, two ladybugs and a caterpillar."

Adam took his first deep breath since encountering Elvis face-to-face and relaxed.

Staring up into the leafy green branches of the oak tree, Emily could just make out the wooden bottom of Jordon's tree house. Ten rungs up the ladder in front of her, banging with a hammer and muttering to himself, was Adam. As soon as he had recovered from the shock of meeting Elvis, he had handed her the pile of wallpaper and renovation books, strapped on a tool belt that had been lying by the front door, and headed to the backyard. Jordon had been right on his heels.

She had placed the books on the kitchen table and followed him out to the huge oak tree, demanding to know what he thought he was doing. His reply had astounded her. He was giving Jordon a birthday present; he was going to revamp the tree fort. She had stood at the bottom of the ladder glaring up into the tree and demanded that he come down immediately. The only one that had descended the ladder had been Jordon. He had been carrying two backpacks crammed with all his toys that had been up in the fort. Whatever Adam had planned, he wanted it to be a surprise for Jordon, and had ordered her son down.

Jordon had sat at the picnic table for the last half hour, staring at the huge oak tree as if a miracle were taking place up in its branches. She didn't like the look of rapture on her son's face, and she definitely didn't like Adam barging into her backyard and taking command of the tree fort. The only way to stop him was to climb the ladder and confront him. She had been working on building up her courage for the last twenty-nine minutes. So far it hadn't budged much above the terrified stage, but her knees had stopped knocking together. Now they were just trembling balls of Jell-O.

She couldn't allow Adam to revamp the fort for Jordon. It was too much. Too personal. Too darn daddyish, if there was such a word. Who did Adam think he was, Mr. Birthday-Wish-Come-True? Just because he happened to have been *her* birthday wish didn't mean he had to become Jordon's. It was only going to hurt her son more when Adam walked away. She grabbed hold of the ladder and started to climb.

By the time her head and upper body emerged through the branches and leaves and entered through the floor of the tree house, she was shaking so badly, she could barely keep her balance on the wooden slat beneath her feet. She grabbed hold of the flooring and used every ounce of strength left in her body to haul herself up into the fort. Hard wood bit into her bare legs as she lay there motionless, willing the dizziness to go away. With a stern silent lecture, she berated herself for her foolishness. She was no higher than the second floor of her house, and she didn't panic every time she went up there. She even periodically went up into the attic and she was perfectly fine, as long as she didn't look out any of the windows. Why should Jordon's fort be any different?

She closed her eyes and felt the coolness of the wood beneath her hands and legs. She was safe.

"Em, are you all right?"

She silently groaned and kept her eyes closed. She knew her appearance wouldn't have gone unnoticed by Adam. She had been praying that his back would be toward the opening when she managed to get up into the fort. Now that the roaring in her ears had diminished to a low clamor of nerves, she noticed that his hammering and muttering had stopped at her arrival. She swallowed hard and whispered, "I'm fine."

Adam laid down his hammer and shifted closer to her. "You don't look fine."

She opened her eyes and glared at him. "How kind of you notice." She kept her gaze pinned on him as she maneuvered herself into a sitting position, far away from the opening in the floor. She purposely kept herself from looking toward the two openings that acted as windows.

Adam continued to frown at her. "Jordon told me you never come up here."

"Did he tell you why?"

"No, so I'm gathering he doesn't know about your fear of heights."

"Is it that obvious?"

"Only to someone who witnessed your entrance." His frown turned into a small smile. "What is so important that you had to come all the way up here to tell me instead of yelling from below? I could hear you just fine from up here."

"My neighbors could hear me just fine, too, Adam. You had managed to tune me out completely. If I had yelled any louder, Mitzi would have come a-running to see if I needed any help getting you out of my tree."

"Don't worry, Em, she never could have climbed the ladder in those shoes she wears."

"You noticed her shoes?" Here she had thought Adam had been totally immune to Mitzi's overstated charms.

"Any woman who wears four-inch heels shaped like ice picks wants her shoes noticed, Em." Adam flashed her his killer smile. "I was just obliging."

She sat up straighter and scowled at him. "Men!"

He chuckled, sliding closer to her on the floor. "Good, your color is back to normal." He reached out and tenderly cupped her cheek. "Don't scare me again like that, Em. You had me worried there for a moment."

She felt the heated flush as it swept up her cheeks. He had been commenting on Mitzi's shoes just to get a rise out of her, and it had worked. She lowered her gaze and encountered his bare chest. She had been so caught up in her fear of heights that she hadn't noticed he had taken off his T-shirt. His chest was golden bronze and just as incredible as she remembered.

Lord, how she remembered that chest.

"Em?"

She quickly glanced away from the tempting sight of soft brown curls and tantalizing skin. "I can't let you revamp, renovate, or whatever it is you're doing to Jordon's tree house, Adam. It's too much." She shrugged. "You know, it's too much for a kid's birthday. A kid you hardly know."

Adam looked guilty. "Maybe I'm not doing it all for Jordon, Em."

"Who else are you doing it for?" Surely he wasn't doing it for her. She would rather see the fort torn down than fixed up. She had a common mother's fear that her son was going to fall out of the tree and break his neck.

"Me, Em, I'm doing it for me. I feel bad for crashing Jordon's party without a present."

"You didn't even know there was a party going on."

He toyed with the wooden handle of the hammer for a moment. "When I was little, I always wanted a tree house. There were plenty of trees in our yard, but there was no one to help me. The only tools my father would hold were the ones that came with the operating room. The nannies and housekeepers were all too refined to be scrambling up a tree with me. By the time I could handle the tools by myself, I was too old for tree houses."

Sympathy rushed through her. How could she ask him to stop now? Jordon loved this fort and Adam needed to fix it for him. Every little boy deserved his own private fort, even if the little boy was thirty-six. "Maybe just a little touch-up wouldn't hurt."

He grinned and moved even closer. His jeans rubbed against her bare legs. "I was thinking of screening in the windows and adding a trapdoor to the opening. Maybe a coat of paint. Some shingles and a pulley system so the kids don't have to carry anything up the ladder when they climb."

She chuckled and held up her hands. "I said 'a little touch-up,' not a complete overhaul that would increase my property value and my taxes." Her gaze once again encountered his bare chest less than two feet away. She could now detect the slight dampness of perspiration clinging to the brown curls. Curls that had wound their way around her fingers when she had stroked that chest.

"Every one of those improvements is for Jordon's safety, Em."

She wasn't paying much attention to what he was saying, but she did hear the words "Jordon's safety" and smiled. Adam cared about her son. "Really?"

He lowered his head and whispered, "Really." He leaned in closer and seemed to be studying her mouth when something else caught his attention. She watched as his eyes widened in surprise, but she didn't turn in the direction of the window. She didn't want to know what had put that strange expression on his face. "Em, don't look now, but I think we have a visitor."

"Who?"

"It's a what, not a who."

"What is it?" Please don't let it be a snake!

Adam tilted his head to one side and studied the creature. "It's a glittering blue cat."

Emily turned her head and grinned. "Adam, meet Leonardo."

"This is one of your cats? Where in the world did you find a glittering blue cat?"

"He's not really glittering, Adam. The tips of his hair are silver and they appear to be shining because of the way the sun is catching his fur."

"So why is he blue?"

"He's a Russian blue, and his coat is bluish gray." She wiggled her fingers and said "Pssss" to the cat. Leonardo gracefully jumped in through the window, turned up his nose at Adam, and pranced his long sleek body over to her. The cat allowed her to scratch him between the ears before heading back out the window and into the tree without giving Adam a second glance.

Adam watched him leave in wonder. "What does Michelangelo look like?"

"Exactly the same, only more arrogant."

"You've got to be kidding! I've never seen a cat look more superior."

She chuckled. "Wait until you meet his big brother."

Emily didn't want to talk about cats, though. She could smell Adam's aftershave and the musky scent of physical labor. Her gaze roamed his chest, the strong column of his throat, and his square jaw. He seemed to be having difficulties breathing as she swayed toward him. His mouth looked so tempting. She wanted to kiss him again to see if her memory had done him justice.

Every bone in her body melted like Velveeta cheese in the microwave as he cupped her cheek and stared into her eyes. Hunger darkened his eyes so that she could no longer tell where his pupils ended and the irises began.

"Can I, Em?"

Could he what? Renovate the tree house? Steal the family silver? Kiss her? Please let it be kiss her! It didn't matter what he wanted, she would gladly allow him to do it. "Yes."

He leaned forward and claimed her mouth in a kiss that was sweet as heaven and hot as Hades. She wrapped her arms around his neck and deepened the kiss. It didn't matter where they were. She was safe within his arms. It was as if she had never left them.

The cool wood floor met her back as Adam's body heated her front. Her fingers danced their way up his back and across his shoulders. She bit his lip and was rewarded with his deep moan and the slight squeezing of his hand as it traveled from her waist to her breast.

His thick arousal bulged against his jeans, and she instinctively parted her thighs. Her hands pulled him closer as she arched her back. She wanted to feel all of him. She wanted to feel him once again as he surged inside of her. She wanted—

"Mom!" Jordon shouted from the bottom of the tree.

She froze as her son's voice penetrated the sensual fog Adam's kiss had generated. The heat of embarrassment replaced the heat of passion.

Adam lifted himself off and away from her. He looked just as shell-shocked as she felt. She quickly sat up and glanced in the direction of the ladder. The tree house was eight feet by eight feet, twelve feet off the ground, and surrounded by more leaves and branches than a Tarzan movie. So why did she have this strange sensation she had just kissed Adam in a fishbowl?

"Mom!" Jordon called again. "You didn't make Adam stop, did you?"

She heard Adam's soft chuckle behind her, but couldn't make herself turn around and face him. They both knew she wouldn't have called a halt to their lovemaking. Who knew where it would have ended if Jordon hadn't interrupted them? It was a disturbing truth, but the truth just the same. She gave a heavy sigh and yelled back, "No, Jordon, I didn't make Adam stop."

SIX

Adam slid between the cool sheets, pushed aside the latest best-selling murder mystery, and reached for the phone. He needed to hear Emily's voice before he went to sleep. He had just left her and the kids two hours earlier, yet he knew he would have a hard time falling asleep without at least wishing her a good night. He propped himself up against the headboard of his bed and pressed the seven digits.

Telephone calls weren't considered a date.

He had a sinking feeling he was going to run out of excuses pretty quick for simply dropping in on Emily and the kids. How long could it possibly take to renovate one small tree house? How many times could he offer advice on new wallpaper? He needed the late night telephone conversations to keep the lines of communication between them open. Emily hadn't seemed threatened by his phone call last night, just his desire to date her.

The phone never rang twice. It was picked up immediately. "Hello?"

"Hello, Em."

"Adam?"

He smiled at the slight catch in her voice. "Were you expecting someone else?"

"Isn't this the same conversation we had last night?" Her light laugh had to be the reason fiber optics were invented. So he could hear every breath she took. He could practically hear her smile.

"Are you trying to say we're in a rut, Em?"

"You, in a rut? I don't think you've ever been in a rut a day in your life, Adam."

"How would you know what my life has been like?" He was curious as to what she thought about him. Most of their discussions so far had centered on ordinary, everyday things.

"You're an only child to two very dynamic people. You probably lacked for nothing growing up and bordered on being spoiled. You're obviously intelligent and you have a certain air of refinement, so I'll guess private schools, certainly a prep school, then four years at an Ivy League college. I haven't figured out why you didn't follow your parents into the field of medicine, but I'm sure it will come to me. You chose the architectural field because you liked it and are very good at it. Lavender Hall Estates isn't your common, run-of-the-mill housing development. Fitting your highly-successful-at-a-relatively-young-age profile, you're probably worrying already what you can do to top Lavender Hall. You're on the lookout for that next mountain to climb, so to speak." She gave a good-natured sigh. "Sorry, Adam, but I don't see a rut anywhere in there."

She'd hit too many bull's-eyes to count. With the Lavender Hall Estate project firmly in hand and under way, he was on the lookout for the next challenge. The proposed development outside of Baltimore was looking interesting, mighty interesting.

Amazed by her understanding of him in just a short while, he filled in the missing piece and said, "I dislike the sight of blood."

"Excuse me?"

He smiled at the confusion in her voice. "I said I get slightly queasy at the sight of blood. That's why I didn't follow either of my parents into the field of medicine." *Slightly queasy!* That was the polite way of saying that he kissed the floor, usually face first, every time he saw the dark red liquid. Both of his parents had taken it in stride that he wasn't following in their gigantic footsteps and hadn't pushed the issue, for which he was eternally grateful.

"Oh, that explains that. So how did you decide to become an architect?"

"Ugly buildings."

"Ugly buildings?"

"Everywhere I went I saw ugly buildings or hideous houses. You know the kind, same beige siding, same garage door, even the same damn yews planted under the front windows. Nothing had any personality. It was like someone had cloned the houses, and I began to wonder that if someone had done that with the houses, did that mean that the people who lived in them were the same too?"

"How old were you?"

"Ten." He smiled when he heard her small laugh. "I learned over the years that the people weren't cloned, but those damn ugly houses still got to me. Builders only build what's on the blueprints, so to change the houses I had to change the blueprints."

"Logical as well as talented. I'm impressed."

"Thank you, but I'm only logical about certain things."

"What kinds of things?" she asked.

"Work, money, things like that."

"What things aren't you logical about?"

It took longer for him to respond to that question. The answer was highly personal and he wasn't sure how she would react to it. "You, Em. I'm not logical where you are concerned."

The "Oh" that drifted over the telephone wires faded softly. Silence so heavy he was sure it was going to overload the circuits followed.

He waited for her to comment further, and when she didn't he asked, "Is that all you can say, 'Oh'?"

"I'm not sure how I'm supposed to respond, Adam."

"Go with your gut instinct, Em. Then take time to think about it later if you have to."

"Last time I did something that illogical, I woke up in a strange hotel room with a man I knew nothing about."

He could hear the self-reproach and maybe, just

maybe, a tinge of humor in her voice. Was she finally getting over her embarrassment of the evening they had met?

He knew they had to come to terms with the past if they were ever going to have a future. The more he learned about Emily, the more important that future became. He had never felt this way about a woman before. Not even his ex-fiancée.

That was because he loved Emily! He didn't know why he hadn't realized it before, but there it was, as clear as any thought he had ever had. He was in love with Emily. It didn't matter that she had three children. It didn't matter that she lived in a blue nightmare that would have Queen Victoria rolling over in her royal tomb for having her name connected with such an atrocity. It didn't even matter that she didn't date.

He was in love with Amelia Carmela Beaufont Pierce, and he couldn't tell her. She would run so fast and build so many protective walls around herself that he might not be able to reach her the next time. Any woman who wouldn't even consider dating surely would panic at the "L" word, and he wasn't talking lust.

What he needed to do now was to go slow and easy, without taking a step backward. "That works both ways, Em. I woke up with a stranger in my arms also." There it was out on the table for them both to examine. "I've never done anything like that before. In today's world it was a totally illogical thing to let happen."

"So you're illogical, I'm illogical, and what we did was illogical?"

"No, Em, what happened between us was extraordinary. Logic didn't enter into it at all." Who ever said love was logical?

Emily gave a light laugh that didn't hold much humor. "That's something you don't have to tell me."

He grinned. Finally something they agreed upon. "That that night was extraordinary?"

"Not that part." Her weary sigh slipped over the telephone line. "The part about logic having nothing to do with it."

She sounded so disheartened and confused that he had to smile. It was either smile or cry, and he didn't feel like crying, not when his heart was finally coming alive. He wondered if he was the total opposite from her ideal of the perfect man. "Em, can I ask you a personal question?"

"You can ask."

His smile grew. "Fair enough." His voice turned serious and the smile faded. "What was your husband like?" He wanted to know about the man who had captured her young heart tight enough that two years after his death, she still didn't date. She had said the children were the reason she didn't date, and while he believed that to a certain extent, he had a feeling it went deeper than that.

"Ray?" Her voice was hesitant. "Why do you want to know about Ray?"

"I'm curious, that's all. If you'd rather not talk about him, I'll understand."

"No. I mean . . . What do you want to know?"

"Anything you want to tell me." He gave her a moment to respond. When she didn't, he asked, "How did you two meet?"

"My college roommate was dating his younger brother, and we were thrown together on a couple of different occasions. We started dating and then we got married the year after I graduated from Penn State."

So Ray had been her college sweetheart! Adam relaxed. There was nothing unique or extraordinary about that. "What did you go to college for?"

"My degree's in elementary education."

"You're a teacher?" He hadn't thought about what she did for a living. He had assumed she stayed at home with the children. It was a ridiculous assumption, considering it was the nineties.

"Not technically. I substituted for the first two years because I couldn't find a permanent position. Then I had Jordon, then Samantha, and then Christopher. They became more important than a career." She paused, as if she were contemplating how much she should tell him, then she said, "When Christopher starts kindergarten, I'm going back to school and getting my master's."

Adam gave a low whistle. "Ambitious."

"No, just logical." She chuckled as she said that last word. "I'll have a better chance at landing a teaching position with a master's degree than without."

"You're going to go out and work?"

"Probably not for another five years or so. Life insurance and the profits from the sale of our old house and Ray's business won't support us forever, though. Do you have any idea what a college education is going to cost in eleven years?"

Christmas! He'd never thought of it that way. It was an unsettling way to look at life. Emily's life. Her whole existence was being planned around and for her children. He wondered if there was going to be any room left for him in her already crowded life.

A week later Emily drove her minivan into the driveway and wearily shut off the engine. The sights and sounds of summer were driving her crazy. Today's outing to the local pool had been a real zoo. The temperature was nearing the hundred-degree mark and every resident within five miles of the pool had had the same idea. She glanced over at Mitzi, who was sitting in the passenger seat. Mitzi had called her that morning and shamelessly begged for a ride to the pool. Her car was in the shop. "That was fun," Emily said. "What do you want to do for an encore, poke sticks in our eyes?"

The screaming of the six kids in the back of the van drowned out most of Mitzi's reply, but Emily got the gist of it from the few words she had understood; something about selling the kids to a wandering band of gypsies.

"Mom," Samantha whined, "Jordon's getting Holly wet!"

"Am not!" shouted Jordon. "It was Shane squirting his water gun."

Mitzi turned toward the back and held out her hand. "Fork it over, buddy. I told you to empty it at the pool."

"It's empty now, Mom," Shane said.

Mitzi wiggled her fingers and raised one perfectly shaped blond eyebrow. The gun was placed in the palm of her hand before Shane opened the side door and got out.

Jordon, Sam, and Shane's two half sisters followed Shane out of the van and into the backyard. Christopher was sound asleep in his car seat.

"Come on, Shane," Jordon said. "I want to show you what Adam did to my tree fort. It's really cool now!" The boys dashed toward the towering oak.

Mitzi glanced at her. "How is Mr. Tall, Dark, and Gorgeous Buns?"

"Adam's fine." Emily didn't like Mitzi's playful name for Adam, but she couldn't argue with the description. Adam was all that and more, much more. She pocketed her keys and stepped out of the van. She didn't want to discuss Adam with her friend. Mitzi might be a little blind when it came to picking out her own husbands, but she wasn't stupid by any means. Mitzi would pick up on what Emily had been trying to deny to herself for the past week: Adam was becoming much too important to her and the children.

She walked around to the other side of the van and started to hand Mitzi the assorted paraphernalia one needed at the local pool.

Mitzi took the beach chair and leaned it against the rear bumper. "I saw he stopped over again last night."

Emily handed her a mesh tote bag filled with bright plastic pool toys. "He put the finishing touches on Jordon's birthday present and allowed him to finally see it." She gathered the assortment of inflatable rings and damp towels the kids had been sitting on. She handed them to Mitzi, who started to systematically sort them into two piles. "He did a wonderful job on the tree fort. Jordon was so thrilled, we had a hard time getting him to come down to get ready for bed."

Mitzi took the beach bag overflowing with sunblock, snacks, two paperbacks, and assorted essentials and placed it on top of her growing pile. "Speaking of *bed* . . ."

Emily glanced up over the seat she was kneeling behind to reach another wet towel and glared at her neighbor. There was no way she were going to hold a conversation with Mitzi that mentioned Adam and bed in the same sentence. "You honestly don't expect me to dignify that question with a reply, do you?" She knew Adam's almost nightly appearances were causing quite a stir in the neighborhood, but for Mitzi to blatantly come right out and ask was unsettling.

"You can answer it if you want, Emily, but it wasn't a question." Mitzi grinned and nodded toward the driveway behind the van. "It was more like an observation."

Emily glanced out the back window of the van and frowned at the car pulling in her driveway. What in the world was Adam doing there? She looked down at herself and silently groaned. She was wearing a damp flowered bathing suit with a pair of red shorts pulled over it. Because of the heat she hadn't bothered with a T-shirt. Her hair was pulled back into a haphazard ponytail that was stiff with chlorine and sunblock. Her nose was burned and she knew the dozen or so freckles she had tried hiding all her life were out in their full summer glory. Her knees were imprinted with hundreds of tiny marks from kneeling on the carpet of the van. She felt like a damp washrag with every ounce of energy twisted and wrung out of her.

She glanced at Mitzi, who was preening and posing at the side of the van as though she were going to appear on the cover of the *Sports Illustrated* swimsuit edition. Emily would be the first to admit she knew nothing about what men liked in a woman, but if she had to take a guess, Mitzi was displaying it all at the moment. Mitzi wore a low-cut one-piece black bathing suit that clung to every lush curve of her body. She had a Hawaiian print skirt wrapped around her hips, and one side was slit to her hip. Every blond hair on her head was neatly in place and looked as if she had spent the day in a beauty shop. She even had on lipstick!

Emily watched as Adam got out of his car and walked toward Mitzi and the van. Glancing down at the damp Mickey Mouse towel in her hand, she felt like chucking it at Mitzi's or Adam's head, she wasn't sure which. With a disgusted sigh, directed mostly at herself, she started to back her way out of the van.

"Hello, Mitzi," Adam said.

Emily rolled her eyes as Mitzi playfully purred back, "Hello yourself, stranger." She felt Adam's hand on her hip as she stepped backward out of the van, then she straightened and brushed off her knees. She handed the grinning Mitzi her daughter's towel.

"Hi, Em," Adam said.

Emily willed herself not to blush as Adam's gaze took a leisurely tour of her body. Approval of what he saw gleamed in his eyes. Not for the first time, she had to wonder what a man like Adam saw in her. She was a hanging-on-by-her-teeth widow with three small children, a half dozen pets, and a house that was built when Chester A. Arthur was president. Not by hers or anyone else's standards was she considered a prime catch.

His gaze seemed to linger on her legs for an inappropriate amount of time before he asked, "Did I catch you coming or going?"

"We just got home from the pool. What brings you here, slow day at the office?" She took in his attire, frowning. His long-sleeved white shirt was immaculate and his dark gray trousers still held a knife-sharp crease. His black shoes shone with a glossy polish, and not one hair on his head was out of place. At least, she thought, he had loosened his tie, an obviously expensive silk one. His smile was dazzling and sexy, and she felt it down to her toes as memories of their night together came flooding back, as always.

"If the boss can't leave a couple hours early, why be the boss?"

"Boy, a person could be really ignored around you two, couldn't she?" Mitzi complained good-naturedly as she bent over to pick up her straw tote decorated with plastic fruit.

Emily blushed to the roots of her hair. Mitzi wasn't used to being ignored by men, but she seemed to be handling it well. In fact, she looked damned pleased about it. "Sorry, Mitzi. Do you need any help carrying all this stuff?"

"Nope. The kids will help or it will be the last time they go to the pool." Mitzi looked over to where the kids and Wellington were dashing from bush to bush. "Shane! Crystal! Ashley! Let's go, kids. Time to head on home."

Five kids came running across the yard. Jordon and Sam ran directly to Adam. Mitzi started handing her children the toys and towels from the pile. Shane grabbed the blanket his mother handed him. "Mom, you should see Jordon's tree fort. It's really cool. Adam's rad."

Jordon beamed proudly and took a step closer to Adam. Emily noticed the hand Adam placed on her son's shoulder. Being called rad was one of the highest compliments the neighborhood kids could bestow on a person. She would have to take Jordon's and Shane's word for how cool the fort had turned out. Adam had tried to get her to climb back up, but she had steadfastly refused. After what had happened up there the other afternoon and how long it had taken Adam to talk her back down the ladder, there was no way she was repeating that humiliating scene.

Mitzi handed Ashley their three inflatable rings

and grinned at Adam. "Really? I always appreciate a man who knows how to use his hands."

Emily rolled her eyes at such an obvious line. Mitzi was obviously enjoying herself immensely. If Adam's grin was any indication, he seemed to be taking her right in stride. Maybe it was time to remind her friend of her future husband number five. "Mitzi, didn't you tell me Paul was coming for dinner?" Paul Dickerson had the look of an NFL linebacker and probably the appetite to match. Mitzi was going to have to brush up on her cooking skills if she hoped to keep him.

Mitzi grinned. "Emily, I do believe your green is showing." She gave Adam a saucy wink and strolled away. Her three children followed her down the drive, arguing with one another all the way.

Adam chuckled. "You've got to admit she has a certain style."

Emily had to join in with laughter of her own. "You're right about that. Mitzi definitely has a style of her own." She leaned back into the van and smiled at her sleeping son. He was wearing a bright red bathing suit with grinning sharks printed all over it, a pair of flip-flops, and about a gallon of sunblock. His little mouth was open and he appeared to be catching flies. Her heart gave a funny little tug.

Adam glanced over her shoulder at the sleeping boy. "He looks zonked to the world."

"It's hard being two and a half." As she unsnapped the belt on the car seat and reached for him, Adam brushed her arms away.

"I'll carry him in. He's awfully heavy for you."

"I carried him for nine months, I think I can make it thirty feet."

Adam's hands seemed extremely gentle as he picked the sleeping boy up and cradled him against his chest. "I know you could manage, Em. But why should you when I'm standing right here?" He shifted Christopher's weight and grinned as the boy snuggled closer. "See, he trusts me."

"He's covered in sunblock." She frowned at Adam's shirt. "It will probably ruin your shirt."

"The cleaners will get it out, Em." He started walking toward the house. "Where do you want him?"

"On the couch in the living room." She quickly closed the van door and grabbed two tote bags and the wet towels before following Adam. The rest of the stuff could wait until later.

She followed the porch around to the back while Adam carried Christopher inside. She left the tote filled with pool toys on the porch, deposited the canvas bag on the kitchen counter, and dropped the towels on top of the washer. She could hear Sam and Jordon talking softly to Adam in the living room. It was amazing. Sam and Jordon never talked softly, no matter if Christopher was sleeping or not. Adam must have placed some kind of spell over her children.

Emily entered the living room and felt her heart give another odd lurch. Adam had laid Christopher on the couch and was bending over him, tucking his Pooh bear in close to his arm in case he should wake up and want his favorite stuffed animal. It was a sweet gesture. It was a fatherly gesture.

Lord, her mind must be going. She must have stayed out too long in the sun. Adam wouldn't know a fatherly gesture if one sat up and bit him on the behind. He had only tucked in the bear because Jordon or Sam must have told him to.

As Adam straightened and backed away, she said, "Thank you."

He smiled. "My pleasure."

She had to turn away from his smile. Adam really did consider it a pleasure to tuck little Christopher in. She glanced at her youngest. He deserved so much more than what he had ever gotten from his real father. He had been only a few months old when Ray had died, and she could count on one hand the number of times his father had tucked him in.

Emily rapidly blinked back the gathering moisture of memories. A person couldn't change the past, only the future. She looked at Samantha and Jordon, who were still wearing their bathing suits. "Both of you go on up and change." The kids hurried from the room and attacked the stairs like a herd of crazed elephants. Emily stepped out into the hall and called up after them, "And remember to hang up the suits this time. Don't throw them into the tub or on the carpet."

Adam joined her in the hall. "Why don't you go get changed, Em? I'll keep an eye on Christopher."

She had never been so thankful to put on more clothes, even if it was one of the hottest days in history. "I'll be right down." She climbed two steps, then turned back around. "There's some fresh squeezed lemonade in the refrigerator. Help yourself."

"Thanks, I will."

She hurried up the remaining stairs, feeling Adam's gaze on her the entire way.

Twenty minutes later she descended the stairs freshly showered and changed into a clean pair of shorts and a top. She headed for the giggling voices in the living room. Adam was sitting on the sofa with Wellington at his feet. Christopher, who obviously had just awakened, was curled up against him and hugging Pooh. Sam and Holly were sitting on the other end of the couch. Jordon was standing beside Adam thrusting picture after picture into his hands. "And that's me at Dorney Park last summer. And that's Sam and Christopher riding some stupid looking ladybug at Dorney Park last summer. And that's—"

"Jordon, I really don't think Adam wants to see those pictures." She didn't know any man who would want to see a bunch of snapshots of some kids at an amusement park.

"Hey, Mom, guess what?" Jordon said excitedly. "Adam's going to take us out to dinner."

SEVEN

Emily stared out the French patio doors, past the slate patio with its classic umbrella table and chairs, to the acres of green lawn and the small pond beyond. A pair of white swans floated across the glasslike surface. To the right of the pond an empty park bench sat nestled between two weeping willows. The entire area was fenced in for privacy with pine trees. Dozens, possibly hundreds, of pine trees. Each tree was wrapped with miniature white lights. Dusk was approaching and someone had turned on the lights. In an hour the entire view would look like something out of a fairy tale. It was a remarkable view. A view worth a pretty penny, and anyone who could afford to purchase one of the exclusive condos she was standing in could well afford the view. Adam had paid the price.

She never should have agreed to come. Between the kids' pleading and Adam's charm, she had fought a losing battle. Then again, it hadn't been much of a battle. Who could have resisted the lure of not having to cook in a kitchen that had been pushing nearly one hundred degrees? In that sort of heat, fans were a joke. A cruel joke.

A restaurant promised cool relief, and with three kids along, no one in his right mind would consider it a date. She had agreed before she learned that Adam wanted to stop at his home to change. Not only was he overdressed for dinner, but he had managed to get slick sunblock all over his shirt from carrying Christopher. She didn't even want to think about the yellow-orange stain he had gotten on his pants when he helped Jordon feed Elvis his dinner of baby food squash.

She knew Adam needed to change, but she and the kids should have waited in her van. Adam's home only emphasized their differences. The minute she'd walked through the door, she had known it was a mistake. The man owned a white couch! She'd never before met anyone who actually owned a white couch. Stores used them for display purposes just to tease the human population with something they couldn't have. She had quickly steered her three children away from the living room.

What should have been the family room had been converted into a media center that would make even Disney envious. All three children had stood in awe in front of Adam's fifty-two-inch television. Any moment she had expected them to bow down and pay homage to the media god. She had swiftly ushered the children out of that room too.

The children were now safely, at least semi-safely, in what should have been an elegant dining room. Instead of a dining room set, Adam had purchased a pool table. A gorgeous red-cloth-and-teak pool table. Adam had given the kids the balls to roll around on top of the table before he went upstairs to change. The kids were having a riot trying to get the colored balls into the pockets. She just prayed they wouldn't damage or break anything. Their sweet laughter brought a fleeting smile to her face. They appeared to approve of Adam's home.

She glanced at the kitchen and eating area behind her. This was how Adam lived. She couldn't find fault with it. Lord, no one could find fault with his home. It was beautifully decorated, refined, and sparkled with class. Everything gleamed, from the light fixtures to the windows. Not a thing was out of place. There wasn't even a dirty coffee cup in the sink. If she hadn't been told, she would never have guessed anyone even lived here. It looked like a sample condo used to lure the average joe into thinking that if he purchased one, he too would be living in such splendor.

Ray would have loved it. She hated it. No, maybe "hate" was too strong a word. She disliked Adam's house. It wasn't a home. It was a sterile, empty house filled with expensive furniture.

Most people would call her house a rundown money pit. On one level she had to agree. The house needed extensive work on its exterior to bring it back to its former glory. The interior was getting there, slowly. But it wasn't the physical appearance of a house that made it a home, it was what went on inside that counted. Her home was filled with children's laughter, the aroma of fresh baked cookies, and love. Adam's condo probably cost more than what her house was worth, but she wouldn't have traded with him for the world.

Ever since Adam had shown up at Jordon's birthday party, a quiet little voice deep inside her had been whispering some very un-Emily-type dreams. Dreams of forever. Dreams of love. Dreams of not having to walk through life alone. Those dreams had been making it awfully hard to fall asleep each night. But once she did finally drift off to sleep, the dreams changed to hot, erotic fantasies, all with Adam in the starring role. Her body remembered his every touch, while her mind was just beginning to learn who he was.

Nothing, though, had shown her who Adam really was like his house. She should have come here first. Then she would have known they had nothing in common, and those disturbing dreams could have died.

Adam walked into his kitchen and glanced at Emily. She looked sad and lonely standing by herself by the patio doors, staring out into the approaching twilight. He wondered what she was thinking.

He came up behind her, close enough to smell the shampoo she had used earlier, but not close enough to touch. Touching Emily would be a mistake. Once had had her back in his arms he might never let her go. In the reflection of the glass he met her pensive gaze. "What's wrong, Em?" He didn't know what had put the sadness in her soft green eyes, but he would do anything to dispel it.

She shook her head, managed a small smile, and stepped away from the doors. "This is a beautiful house, Adam. I was just admiring your view."

He glanced out the doors to the freshly manicured lawn beyond. The view was spectacular, that was why he had picked this particular condo, but it had been a long time since he'd admired it. He turned back to Emily. "Would you like to get the nickel tour of the rest of the place?" He was really proud of the layout of the condominiums. The design of these buildings had been the first big break his firm had received.

She cringed as Christopher let out a squeal of delight. They heard Jordon whisper harshly, "Christopher, stop that. If Mom sees you doing that, you'll get into trouble."

"I think I'll take a raincheck on the tour," Emily said as she hurried toward the children.

Adam followed her, shaking his head. There wasn't a thing in the poolroom the kids could ruin. Em wouldn't let them have the cue sticks. All they had was a bunch of balls, a rack, and the table. How much trouble could they get into? Christopher's sudden wail of outrage hurried him on.

He stepped into the room and stared in amazement. Jordon and Sam were standing by the table trying to look innocent, while Em was kneeling in front of Christopher. Her low muttering and Christopher's cries reached his ears. He stepped to the side of Emily and stared at Christopher. The little tyke had managed to put the triangular rack over his head, past one arm, and through one leg. Scratch that, he had stepped into the thing with one leg and then put an arm into . . . Oh, hell, he had no idea how Christopher had managed to get himself tangled up in the thing.

"Stop moving, Christopher," Emily said as she tried to wriggle his arm back through the wooden rack.

"Ouch, Mommy, that hurts," Christopher cried as he tried to back away.

Emily caught him before he fell. "Don't move, young man."

Christopher froze. Adam almost smiled at her tone of voice. Marine drill sergeants would be envious of the respect and obedience she commanded without even raising her voice. He watched as she tried to gently maneuver the rack over Christopher's head. She wasn't successful.

The little boy's eyes filled with huge glistening tears.

Adam knelt down and gently turned Christopher toward him, away from Emily. "Hey, Chris, my man, would you like me to help untangle you?"

Christopher glanced at his mother, then at Adam, and slowly nodded.

"Okay, son, here's what I'm going to do. First I'm going to look you over." He studied the wooden triangle and the little body it was wrapped around. "Next step is for you to sit down and curl yourself into a small ball." He helped the boy to sit on the floor. "Then we're going to pull your leg out of here." He carefully eased Christopher's left leg out of the rack. "Then it's a simple process of"—he helped Christopher to stand back up—"pulling the thing over your head and arm." The rack came free and Christopher beamed.

"Thanks, Adam," the boy exclaimed as he threw himself into his mother's waiting arms.

Adam grinned. He loved the way Christopher said his name. He forgot to pronounce the "d," and the "s" in thanks had been a little shaky. "You're welcome, buddy. It would have been awfully hard for you to eat your dinner with that thing wrapped around you."

Jordon and Sam giggled, and Emily smiled her first real smile since entering his house. "Thank you, Adam."

"You're welcome." He ruffled Christopher's hair. His heart flipped over when the boy raised his blond head and smiled at him as if he were a god. A strange lump filled his throat. He had to clear it twice before asking, "Is everybody hungry?"

The children's chorus of "Yes!" was deafening.

Emily tucked the sheet printed with baseball players in around Jordon and kissed him good-night. It was too stiflingly hot to worry about blankets, but Jordon liked to sleep with at least something covering him. "Good-night, hon. See you in the morning." She smoothed his hair and straightened back up.

"Mom?"

"Yes?" Christopher was already asleep in his room,

and Samantha was tucked into her bed with Holly close by. Jordon was the last one she kissed every night. Tonight their nightly routine had taken longer than usual because the children were still pumped up from all the earlier excitement. Not only had Adam treated them to dinner, but they had stopped off for a game of miniature golf. A wonderful, fun-filled family outing. Only problem was, they weren't a family. And she would do herself a world of good if only she could remember that. Tonight it had been hard. Real hard. She could have easily slipped into the fantasy.

"I really like Adam." Jordon nervously played with the edge of the sheet.

Emily forced her expression to remain neutral. She wanted to frown, stamp her feet, and scream. She'd known this was going to happen. "That's nice, Jordon."

His voice got small as if he were unsure how to phrase the next question. "Do you think he likes me?"

The groan that rumbled in her throat stayed there. She took a couple of deep breaths before sitting down on the bed. "I know he likes you, Jordon." She brushed back a lock of his brown hair. The light in the room was off, but the one in the hall sent a stream of light over the bed. "What's really on your mind, hon?"

"Is Adam going to become our dad?"

His hopeful expression nearly broke her heart. Things had been so hectic around the house since Jordon's party that she hadn't found the time to sit down with him and have a mother-to-son talk about stepfathers and wishing for a dad. Or maybe she was just trying to avoid the entire subject while praying it would go away. "I'm afraid not, Jordon."

"But you said he likes me." Jordon looked ready to cry. "He was real nice to Christopher tonight, and when Sam dropped her ice cream cone he didn't yell at her. He went back and bought her a new one."

"I know, hon. But all those things mean he's a nice person, not that he's applying for the position of becoming your dad." She wondered how much she should explain to Jordon. Should she tell him she wasn't interested in taking applicants to fill his father's shoes? That she wasn't looking for a new husband? She wasn't even sure if Jordon connected the fact that for him to get a new daddy, she would have to get a new husband.

"Did you kiss him?"

Shock slammed through her like a freight train. "What did you say?" She had to have heard him wrong. Her seven-year-old son couldn't be asking if she had kissed Adam.

"Did you kiss him?" Jordon chewed on his lower lip, a sure sign that he was thinking about something. "Shane said his mom kisses all his dads. That's how they become his dads."

Emily tried to calm her breathing, but there was no way she could control her pounding heart. She had a dreadful feeling that she didn't want to know what else Shane might have said. Jordon had unknowingly answered one of her questions. He knew that for Adam to become his dad, he would have to be connected with her somehow. The kissing part had thrown her for a moment. But between Sex Education 101, compliments of eight-year-old Shane, and television, it was only natural for Jordon to connect kissing with dads. You couldn't turn on the television without seeing someone kissing someone.

She couldn't tell her son that she had kissed Adam. Groaning silently, she thought of all she had done with the man. But she couldn't lie to Jordon either. What was called for was a diversion tactic. "You don't go around kissing friends, Jordon. Adam is our friend. Yours, mine, your brother's, and your sister's."

"But if you kissed him, that would make him my dad, right?"

"No. It would make him a man I kissed, nothing more. Men and women can kiss without the man's becoming anyone's dad, honey."

"But Shane said—"

"Shane shouldn't be telling you or anyone else who his mother kisses. It's improper." What in the world was Mitzi thinking, letting her son see her kissing those men? No wonder poor Shane was so confused. And his confusion was being relayed back to Jordon! "Now I want you to go to sleep, okay?"

"Is Adam still here?"

"Yes, he's downstairs, but he's going to be going home shortly." Because of Christopher's car seat, they had taken her van to Adam's condo then out to dinner. He had returned with them to the house, and tonight, unlike the other nights, he hadn't been in a hurry to leave when she announced that she had to put the kids to bed. He was waiting for her downstairs in the living room.

"Can you tell him that I said thanks again?" Jordon snuggled deeper into his pillow and yawned. "It was really cool learning how to golf."

She pressed another kiss to his forehead and stood up. "I'll tell him." She didn't have the heart to explain to Jordon that there was a world of difference between miniature golf and the real sport. She stepped into the hallway and partly closed his door so the light didn't hit him directly on the face.

Standing there, she looked at the three bedroom doors, and sighed. What was she going to do now? Tonight had not only been a mistake, it had been a disaster. Jordon wanted her to kiss Adam so that he would become their dad. Samantha had held Adam's hand when he'd bought her a new vanilla ice cream cone after she'd accidentally dropped hers. And Christopher had clung to his leg like cheap polyester the entire evening. Her kids were smitten with Adam, and she couldn't blame them.

Adam had been wonderful, charming, and fun. He seemed to handle the kids like a pro, or maybe it was just dumb luck that he managed to connect on their level. From his performance these last several days, any kid in the world would be thrilled to have him for a dad.

It was a real shame she had to send him packing, and fast. Sighing again, she headed for the stairs.

Adam heard Em's light footsteps coming down the stairs and shut off the television. While she had tucked in the kids, he had turned on the news. It was either watch the local news or go out of his mind worrying. Something was wrong. His plan to woo Emily slowly was falling apart faster than a cheap sweater, and he couldn't seem to find the thread that had begun the unraveling.

Something had changed tonight, but what? He had first noticed it at his condo. But for the life of him he couldn't figure out why his home would have upset Emily.

She walked slowly into the room. Her gaze connected with the blank television set, Wellington sleeping by his feet, and the walls. Everything but him. He knew a bad omen when he saw one. He patted the cushion next to him on the couch. "Sit, Em. I think we need to talk."

She sat, but she put as much distance between them as the couch would allow. "You're right. We need to talk." She stared down at her hands for a long moment.

He sighed. The ball was back in his court. "You've been acting kind of strange all evening, Em. Want to tell me what's bothering you?"

Her hands must have grown another set of fingers by all the attention she was giving them. When she finally spoke, her voice was low and throaty. "I don't think you should come around anymore, Adam."

His rapid heartbeat slammed on its brakes, and he swore it came to a complete halt. He'd known he wasn't going to like it, but he hadn't figured she'd be this brutal. Just stop coming around! It would be easier to give up breathing than to stay away from Emily. "Would you like to tell me why?"

"The kids are really becoming attached to you, Adam. Jordon is harboring this dream that birthday wishes do come true."

He knew what Jordon's wish had been, and he wasn't running in horror as Emily obviously was betting he would. "Jordon's a good kid, Em. You should be very proud of him."

She glared at him. "Sam wants to know if she can rename her white angelfish Adam, and Christopher wanted you to read to him tonight instead of me." She bit her lower lip and took a few calming breaths. "I don't want them to become attached to you, Adam. So I'm asking you very nicely not to visit us any longer."

He saw the fear enter her eyes and was taken aback. What was she afraid of? He hadn't given her one reason to fear him physically. Was she really afraid the kids were becoming too attached to him, or was she afraid she was becoming too attached? "What are you really afraid of, Em?"

"Nothing." Her chin rose a notch, but she didn't meet his gaze.

"You're afraid of something, and while it might partly have to do with the kids, it's not the real reason you don't want to see me anymore." He was losing her. He could see it in the stubborn tilt of her chin. This heat between them couldn't be all on his side. She had to feel it too. He had to show her the heat. He was left with only one option.

He slid across the sofa and pulled her into his

arms. Her eyes filled with dread and something else, possibly desire. He slowly lowered his head and brushed her lips with his own. Sweet fire blazed to life. The fire was instantaneous, consuming, and insatiable. He had felt and fed this fire only twice before in his life. The night he first met Emily, and that afternoon in the tree house.

He could feel his arms tremble as he pulled her closer and deepened the kiss. Her mouth opened beneath his and he lost himself to the flames. Tongues danced to the primitive rhythm as old as time. Hands reacquainted themselves with the length of her back and the silky softness of her hair.

He groaned her name as she pulled him closer and lightly nibbled on his lower lip. Her plump breasts were crushed against his chest, and he could feel her one hand pressed to the back of his head while the other . . . Lord help him, her other hand was gripping his thigh. It had landed there when he hauled her into his arms, but she should have moved it. Five fingers branded his thigh. *Please let her move it! Preferably higher, and higher . . .*

Adam broke the kiss because he knew he couldn't control it any longer. The heat was too intense, too tempting. He looked into her startled eyes and knew. "You felt it too, Em. Don't deny it." He gently stroked her lips with his thumb. They were moist, slightly swollen, and incredibly tempting. "There's something very special and rare between us, Em. It's too special to be ignored."

He put a couple of inches of space between their bodies. "So what are you going to do about it?"

Emily moved back farther and wrapped her arms around herself. "Nothing, Adam. I'm going to do nothing about it."

He frowned as she stood up and walked to the window to stare out into the night. He wondered if staring out windows was a habit of hers. As she had at his condo, she looked so alone standing there, and he wanted to go to her and give her comfort. But he sensed she was coming to some kind of decision. A decision that concerned them.

Without turning from the window, she asked, "You've worked very hard to get where you are, haven't you?"

"Yes." What else could he say? Only a moron would think he'd achieved everything he had by pure luck or laziness. Emily wasn't a moron.

"That wasn't really a fair question, Adam. I knew the answer. You're obviously very good at what you do and you enjoy the work. That's something to be proud of. A lot of people skim by the work aspect of life and then wonder why they never achieve anything. You don't mind paying the price, and I have to admire that in you. I understand what drives a man to push himself harder, to sacrifice more, to reach for a dream." She turned from the window and looked at him, her expression sad. "I was married to such a man."

"Are you comparing your husband's advertising agency with my architectural firm?"

"In a way, yes. Ray came from a low-income home.

He was driven to succeed in business. Being a top em-ployee wasn't enough; he had to own his own business. He had to get the biggest and best accounts. He had to belong to the best country club and drive the newest car. His house had to be in the right neighborhood, his clothes from the right store, and his family had better be picture perfect.

"Don't get me wrong, Adam. Ray loved me and the children. And we loved him in return. But to reach his dream of what he thought life should be, he had to make sacrifices."

"And what he sacrificed was you."

"He sacrificed his family, not just me." Emily glanced at the silver picture frame on the fireplace mantel. The photo inside had been taken two months before Ray had died. It was a seemingly casual family photo of Ray, herself, and the three children, but there had been nothing casual about the shot. The expensive photographer Ray had hired was good at what he did, posing them all exactly yet making them all look natu-ral.

"Ray worked seven days a week, if not in the office, then on the golf course. His days were long, with most ending in business dinners and discussions that went on for hours.

"At first I thought he might have a mistress stashed somewhere, but he didn't. Sometimes I wished he had. Another woman, I would have known how to fight, but not this dream to succeed. How do you take some-one's dream, someone's ambition? He wanted what was best for his family, and he honestly thought he was doing the right thing by only providing us financial support."

"Didn't you ever tell him how you felt?"

"Many times." She looked away from the family photo. "Once I even threatened to leave him. He promised he would cut down on his hours, become more of a husband and father. But there was always one more deal, one more client to satisfy. He said as soon as he 'made it' he would be able to take some time off, relax and enjoy his family. I believed him because deep down inside I knew he thought he was doing the best thing for his family."

"How did Ray die, Em?"

"Heart attack. He had just turned thirty-eight, and one day he was sitting at his desk in his prestigious office in center city Philadelphia, putting together the finishing touches to another great ad campaign, and he fell out of his chair. He had died before he even hit the floor. There was an autopsy which showed that he had had a defective heart all along, he just never knew it."

"I'm sorry, Em." Lord, Adam thought, he couldn't imagine what she must have gone through.

"So am I, Adam, but I can't change the past." She walked away from the window to stand directly in front of him. "I also won't repeat the same mistakes from the past. You're like Ray, Adam, a type A personality. Your work is your life and I can't find fault with that. But I also know I can't compete with it. I can only wish you all the luck and success in the world." She walked toward the front door as if she fully expected him to follow. He did simply because she'd walked out of the room and he wasn't done talking to her. Not nearly done.

Emily stood by the front door. "The children and I thank you for a wonderful time tonight."

"You expect me to walk out that door and not come back, don't you?"

"Yes, that's exactly what I expect, Adam."

He didn't want to leave, but Emily didn't appear as if she could handle any more resistance. She looked ready to crumble. She also looked as though she wasn't ready to listen to him. "I'll leave, Em. But I'm not staying away." He brushed her a fleeting kiss across her mouth. "While you've been playing second fiddle to some man who didn't know how to prioritize his life, I've been living in the real world. What's between us is special, Em. I'm not about to walk away from it." He shoved open the screen door and stepped out onto the porch. "And I'm not about to let you, either."

EIGHT

Monday afternoon Adam stood in his office and contemplated the traffic making its way along Duke Street. In the seven years since he had purchased the historic Federal-style home and converted it into his offices, the city of Lancaster had grown by more than leaps and bounds. The entire downtown had been renovated. His firm had had the honors of helping to design some of the more prestigious buildings. Lancaster was trying to hold on to its heritage while moving toward the twenty-first century. He thought it was succeeding better than most other cities.

The construction crew he had hired was wrapping up the renovations to the third floor of his building. Within the next two weeks the offices up there would be ready to be occupied. That morning he had hired one of the architects to fill one of the offices. Two more promising candidates were scheduled for interviews the latter part of the week.

His business was keeping pace with the city. He should be ecstatic. He wasn't.

He was proud of his business and the people who worked for him. They were all excellent employees and extremely talented. He had handpicked every one of them, from the more experienced to the youngsters fresh out of college who were dreaming about changing the world, one building at a time. At one time he had thought this was all he could possibly want out of life. A business of his own, a career he loved, and both respect and prestige in the architectural community. It was everything he had always dreamed of.

So why wasn't it enough?

Emily! The answer came swift and sure. Until he had met Emily, he had been content. He had thought he had it all. Boy, was he mistaken. His gut was telling him that without Emily, he had nothing.

He had given her a few days to contemplate her decision not to see him again. The weekend had been hell. He usually spent his weekends either working, catching up on trade magazines, or on rare occasions hitting eighteen holes at the country club. That weekend he hadn't been able to concentrate on work, and golf had held absolutely no appeal. Emily's late husband had played golf.

Sunday he had visited his parents. His father had been at his country club with his cronies, making the most of the beautiful day. His mother had been in her office, planning some annual fall fund-raiser and making final adjustments on the summer fund-raiser scheduled for the next month. At seventy-six Celeste

Young's eyes might not be sharp enough to allow her to spend hours a day hunched over a microscope, but that didn't stop her from trying to conquer cancer. She spent an incredible amount of time and energy raising funds to support the ongoing research.

When Adam had shown up, though, his mother had pushed aside her fund-raising work and given him some motherly—or was it womanly—advice. *Tell Emily the truth*, she'd said. *Tell her about your broken engagement to Georgia. Tell her you're also scared and have no idea where any of this is going to lead. But most importantly, tell her you love her.*

Celeste hadn't so much as batted an eye two months earlier when he had told her he'd called off the wedding to Georgia De Witt. Sunday, however, she'd displayed an amazing amount of curiosity about Emily, especially after he'd dropped the little bombshell about Emily having three children. For the rest of time that he was there, she had stared at him as if *he* were an organism under a microscope.

All the previous night he had thought about Emily and his mother's advice. What did he have to lose? It couldn't get any worse than Emily barring the door to him, which she was ready to do. The more he thought about it, the madder he became. Emily had unfairly condemned him for another man's crime.

He rubbed the back of his neck and glanced around his office. A dozen files and just as many blueprints were spread out over the table in the corner, all needing his attention. For the first time since opening the doors of Young Architects and Design, he couldn't get enthused about the work. He didn't want to be there. He wanted to be in Emily's kitchen drinking fresh squeezed lemonade and munching on warm chocolate chip cookies. He wanted to help Jordon feed Elvis his dinner and fix the loose wheel on Holly's baby stroller for Sam. He wanted to carry Christopher on his shoulders and toss Wellington his chewed-up red rubber ball. He wanted to help Emily strip that god-awful rooster wallpaper from her dining room walls. But most of all, he wanted to join Emily in her bed and make love to her until the ache went away.

Adam closed his eyes and willed the desire to lessen. He needed at least a semblance of control. He had been confusing his employees with his distracted attitude and short temper. Even his own secretary, who had been with him since the beginning, was giving him strange looks.

This had to end.

He had given Emily enough space and time to think things through. He reached for the phone book and quickly turned to the listing for florists in the yellow pages. It was time for him to take some action. He wasn't about to lose Emily because of a ghost from her past. Not even if that ghost had been her husband and the father of her children.

Emily stared at the vase filled with a dozen long-stemmed white roses and knew she was going to let Adam in when he showed up in a few minutes. The flowers had been delivered late in the afternoon with only a simple note attached: *Have the kids in bed by ten. Adam.* At first she had been insulted at such a blatant disregard for her children, but then she had given the note some thought. Adam was only doing what she wanted. Tonight when he came by, the children would all be tucked into their beds, and she wouldn't have to worry about them falling deeper in awe of Adam.

His absence this past weekend hadn't gone unnoticed by the children. Christopher had asked at least twice a day where Adam was, Samantha had wanted her to call him and invite him to the local pool when they went on Saturday, and Jordon . . . Jordon was going to be a problem. Her elder son had been scowling at her all weekend. Jordon thought she was behind Adam's disappearance. What could she say? He was right.

She had practically thrown Adam out of the house the other night and told him not to come back. He had left with the promise that he'd be back, and she had been on edge the past several days. She had jumped every time the phone rang or someone knocked on the door. All for nothing.

The bouquet of roses was the first contact she had had from Adam in over five days. The fragrance of the sweet blooms melted her heart. It had been so long since anyone had cared enough to send her flowers. In truth it had been so long since she'd cared about anyone besides the children and her extended family. Adam made her feel alive, and it scared her.

Her fear had prodded her to push him out the door and out of her life. It now appeared Adam wasn't about to be pushed. She bent over a delicate white bloom and inhaled. A small smile teased her mouth. In fact, it appeared Adam was about to do some pushing of his own. A dozen long-stemmed white roses was one hell of a shove.

She didn't know what scared her more, that Adam would break her heart or the consequences any relationship with him would have on her children. Knowing Shane and his two half sisters as she did, she guessed there were going to be a lot of unresolved problems in Mitzi's family. But did that mean that her children would suffer the same ordeals? She no longer believed that. Maybe she'd never believed it and had only used that as an excuse to hide from her own fears. It was a disturbing thought. Was she actually hurting her children by not allowing a father figure into their lives?

Jordon obviously wanted a dad or he wouldn't have been wishing for one on his birthday. Little boys naturally wanted someone to play catch with, someone to teach them how to throw a football, someone to take them fishing who didn't try to bait the hook with her eyes closed. She could give her children all her love and time, teach Jordon to toss a football, and even take them fishing. But she could never be their dad. She would always be their mother.

She gave a start as a car pulled into the driveway. Adam was there. By the chiming of the grandfather's clock in the front parlor, he was right on time. Time for what? She hadn't a clue. Nor was she ready.

She forced herself to relax and walk toward the

front of the house when he lightly tapped on the door. She hadn't bothered to change from the sleeveless cotton dress she had slipped on after returning from the pool with the kids. There wasn't an enticing feature to the high-waisted, scooped-neck, full-skirted dress. The nicest thing anyone could say about it was that the light green color matched her eyes. She knew how comfortable and light the dress was in the summer heat. The only jewelry she had on was a gaudy but precious sunflower pin Jordon had given her last Christmas.

Her fingers were ringless, as they had been for a while. Six months after Ray had died, she had taken off her wedding ring. She hadn't felt right about moving into her grandmother's house and starting a new life while wearing the gold band. Her large engagement ring was safely tucked into her jewelry box to be worn on special occasions. Since special occasions were few and far between, she rarely saw the flawless diamond.

The only visible sign that she had taken any time to prepare for Adam's late visit was her hair. She had French-braided it into a soft, sophisticated style.

The brass doorknob felt cool in the palm of her hand as she opened the door. Adam stood on the porch looking deliciously handsome in a short-sleeved yellow polo shirt and navy twill pants. His hair was slightly ruffled, as if he had just run his fingers through it.

"Hello, Em."

Her heart gave a funny little lurch at his fleeting

smile. "Hi." She held the door open wider. "I gather
you want to come in."

He glanced at the fat cushioned chairs nestled in
the shadows of the porch. "We could sit out here if
you want."

She didn't trust herself to sit in the dark with
Adam. It would be too easy to surrender to temptation. To surrender to her dreams. She physically
wanted Adam. There was no mistaking the passion
that burned between them. But like the old Rolling
Stones song went, you can't always get what you want.
She turned away from the tempting sight and stepped
farther into the hall. "Why don't we use the kitchen."
She'd be safe in the kitchen with its cheery walls and
bright lights.

Adam followed her into the house and closed the
door behind him. As he walked past the opening into
the living room, he spotted the flowers he had sent
sitting on top of the television. Michelangelo and Leonardo, the feline blue duo, were both sleeping on the
back of the sofa. Wellington had yet to make his appearance. Some protection he was! Anyone could
stroll right in and do anything they wanted to Emily
or the children. It was a frightening thought.
"Where's Wellington?"

"Sleeping on the patio, why?" She walked over to
a glass-fronted cabinet and took down two glasses.
"Want some iced tea or lemonade?"

"Lemonade, thank you." He walked to the screen
door overlooking the slate patio and stared out. Sure
enough, Wellington was asleep out there, lying on his

back. The one-hundred-pound gray, white, and black fur ball was sprawled less then three feet from the door. If the dog hadn't been so damn lumpy, someone might have mistaken him for a rug. "Why didn't he hear my car?" The driveway was on the side of the house. Surely the dog must have heard him pull up.

Emily filled the glasses with ice from the dispenser in the refrigerator door. "He's deaf in his right ear and can't hear too well out of his left."

Adam continued to stare at the snoring mountain of fur. "You're kidding, right?" Even with him speaking less than four foot away and the racket Emily had made filling the glasses with ice, Wellington hadn't moved so much as a paw.

Emily poured lemonade into the glasses and carried them over to the table. "Why would I lie about something like that?" She sat down and slid one glass over to the empty space beside her. "He only has about ten percent hearing in his right ear and maybe, if he's lucky, fifty percent in his left. It's kind of hard for the vet to know exactly, but that's his best estimate."

Adam turned away from the screen door and took the seat next to Emily. In the center of the table sat a huge pewter pitcher overflowing with sunflowers. Huge silk sunflowers. The centerpiece was just the right touch to the pine table with its bow-back chairs. Emily had a knack for turning a house into a home. It was one of the first things he'd noticed about her house. It felt lived in.

Her home conveyed the same feeling as his oldest

pair of jeans. They were well worn and over time the denim had become soft and supple. There was nothing like coming home from work, stripping off his suit and tie, and slipping into those jeans. It was a pleasure he didn't experience too often. Now he had to wonder why.

He picked up his glass and took a sip. He noticed the dark circles beneath Emily's eyes and the slight trembling of her fingers. She didn't look as though she'd been sleeping any better than he had. Maybe she did miss him a bit. The trembling of her fingers tugged at his heart. The last thing he wanted was to make her nervous. He stayed with the safe subject of her dog. "How does Wellington guard the house if he's deaf?" To his way of thinking, it was ridiculous to have a dog that couldn't protect the house, especially a dog Wellington's size.

"Wellington a guard dog?" Emily burst out laughing. She glanced between him and the screen door, where the dog was barely visible in the light spilling through the door. "I can see the headlines now: 'Burglar Licked to Death by Zealous Dog.'"

Her rich laughter floated over him like a spring shower, fresh and invigorating, the nourishment for new life. This was the Emily he had come to find, not the silent, polite woman who had answered the door. He grinned as her laughter faded to chuckles that skimmed up his spine. He sighed in relief as she relaxed into her chair.

"So if he isn't for protection, what purpose does he serve?" He once again glanced out the screen door and grinned when a lightning bug landed on Wellington's nose. At least he thought it was the dog's nose. With all that hair, it was hard to tell. Wellington never moved as the bug lit up, went dark, and lit up once more.

"Why does he have to have a purpose?" Emily asked. "Can't we have a dog just to have a dog?"

He had never looked at it that way before. He hadn't been allowed a cat when he was growing up because his mother was allergic to cat hair. The dog he had wanted when he was about Jordon's age was vetoed because his father said they already had one of the best security systems money could buy. He couldn't imagine what his mother's reaction would have been if he had asked for an iguana.

He had been allowed an aquarium in his room because both of his parents felt the sight of fish swimming around in twenty gallons of water would have a relaxing effect on him. They had been right. Now he wondered whatever had happened to that old tank with its scuba diver and treasure chest filled with shiny baubles.

Adam glanced once again at Wellington. "Considering what it must cost you to feed him, I presumed he served some purpose besides shedding hair all over the house."

"He loves us, that's purpose enough."

The dog loved them, so he would be pampered and praised like a king for all his doggie years to come. Adam had to wonder if the same principle would hold true with a man. Would Emily welcome him into her life simply because he loved her? An intriguing thought!

He stared into her green eyes and felt the pull of her heart. Did the tides feel the same helplessness against the moon? This pull. This feeling of inevitability that he had to go wherever she led. Was this what love was all about?

A small smile played across his mouth. "He's one lucky dog, Em."

Emily glanced at the dog, then back to Adam. "Maybe this family's the one that is lucky."

He studied the moisture beading on the outside of his glass. "Maybe." The cool drops of condensation coated his fingertips.

Emily could tell whatever he was thinking was lying heavy on his mind. She wondered if she should tell him she was having second thoughts—heck, she was having third and fourth thoughts—about sending him away. She didn't have a lot of experience with men, only her late husband and Adam, but she knew one very important thing. Whatever was happening between Adam and herself was unique. The night in the hotel room was just a sensual blur. She was afraid to trust her memories, to know what was real and what was her imagination. But the other night when Adam had taken her in his arms and kissed her, she had known. Her memories of that one night couldn't compare to the real thing.

Adam Young was one very special guy and she'd be insane to toss him out of the house a second time. She had always been proud of her cool, calm handling of herself. At least, she always had until Adam walked into her life bringing passion with him and scattering chaos in his wake. If Adam hadn't sent the flowers that afternoon, she doubted if she would have held out another day before calling him.

She wanted that chaos. She wanted Adam to haul her into his arms and kiss her again. She wanted to feel alive.

Adam didn't look as though he were ready to haul her or anyone else into his arms. By the worried look on his face, she wasn't sure if she wanted to know what was on his mind. "Want to tell me why you stopped over?"

"You need to know, Em."

"About?"

"My fiancée."

"Your fiancée?" Oh good God, Adam was engaged! "You're engaged?"

"I meant to say my *ex*-fiancée, Georgia De Witt."

Emily allowed air to reenter her lungs. It was okay. He wasn't engaged to another woman.

Adam smiled hesitantly before continuing. "I'd known Georgia for years. We traveled in the same social circles and we were constantly running into each other at this event or that fund-raiser. One day her escort had to back out of an arrangement and she called to ask if I would fill in. I said yes. She hated to go alone to functions because everyone started fixing her up with this cousin or that old roommate from college. I could sympathize because I usually ran into the same type of embarrassing situations. It seemed quite natural for Georgia and I to become a pair."

Emily gave him an encouraging smile. She could see where the two single people had gravitated toward each other to keep the matchmaking wolves at bay.

"After about a year," he went on, "everyone started speculating when the wedding would be. I looked at Georgia, she looked at me, and we both said why not."

"Why not?" Emily was appalled. Who ever heard of getting engaged because of a "why not"?

"We were both in our thirties, single, and we had a lot of friends and associates in common. I always figured I would marry one day. Georgia possesses all the fine qualities a man could want in a wife. I assumed I was what she was looking for in a husband."

"What about love? Didn't you love her?" She was beyond appalled. Adam, the man of her dreams, had decided to marry a woman because they shared the same friends!

"Did I love her the way a man should love the woman he's about to take for his wife?" He shook his head. "No. I love Georgia like a dear friend." He smiled slightly. "The last time I spoke to Georgia, she was still quite miffed at me because we hadn't made love."

Emily knew it was rude and extremely bad mannered, but she had to ask. "Not ever?" This was the nineties, after all. No one expected the bride to be a blushing virgin on her wedding night. Especially a bride who was in her thirties and who had been engaged to Adam. Adam was the sexiest man who'd ever walked on land.

"Don't sound so shocked, Em. I told you that I'd never before done anything like what we did the night we met. I didn't believe in passion." He shook his head at her look of incredulity. "I didn't say that I was a virgin, for Pete's sake. I just thought Georgia would appreciate the courtesy of waiting for our wedding night."

She had to wonder exactly what type of woman this Georgia was that Adam hadn't felt any desire for her. He thought this paragon of the social set would appreciate the courtesy of his foregoing sex. She and Ray hadn't waited for their wedding night. And she and Adam had barely waited until they were safely behind a locked door. She guessed she wasn't the type to appreciate the courtesy. "Did she appreciate it?" It was a strange question to ask, all things considered. But she was curious.

"As it turns out, no. Georgia is a gorgeous petite blonde with china blue eyes that could drive men insane. She's witty, intelligent, and has a heart the size of Texas."

Emily decided right then and there that she hated Adam's ex-fiancée.

"For some reason that totally escapes me," he continued, "she now feels undesirable because we didn't make love. She's assured me that she isn't in love with me, but she doesn't believe for one minute that it's worked out for the best that we didn't make love."

She definitely didn't like Georgia, Emily thought,

but she was curious about one thing. "Who broke the engagement?"

"I did when I realized I didn't love her the way a husband should love his wife. It would have been a mistake. Georgia deserved better."

Adam also deserved better, Emily thought, but he was too much of a gentleman to say it. It must have taken a lot of courage to end the engagement. "How did Georgia take the news?"

"She took it very well." Adam sipped his lemonade. "I think she had come to the same conclusion, but she just hadn't worked up the nerve to tell me. The split was mutual, but her brother took exception to me breaking his sister's heart." His hand went to his right eye. "Morgan De Witt is very, and I do mean very, fond of his baby sister."

Emily cringed. Adam didn't have to say another word. She could figure out what must have happened. Poor Adam, doing the honorable thing and being socked in the eye for it. She gave him a sympathetic smile. "How long ago was that?"

"What?"

"How long ago did this De Witt fellow pop you one?"

"About five minutes after I told Georgia I couldn't marry her."

Emily frowned. Adam was being evasive all of a sudden. Of course Georgia's brother would react immediately. Punching the man who you thought had broken your sister's heart wasn't something you put off doing, like spring housecleaning. It was a passionate response, not an intellectual one. "I meant, how long ago did you and Georgia go your separate ways?"

Adam's gaze locked with hers. She couldn't understand the pleading message his eyes were sending. Why would Adam plead for understanding?

He cleared his throat twice before saying, "I broke our engagement the week after I met you, Em."

NINE

Adam knew he was in trouble by the look on Emily's face. Deep trouble. Common sense had told him Emily wasn't going to take that bit of news very well, but he had been left with little choice. He had to tell her now, or chance being caught in a lie later. If he was going to build a relationship with Emily, it had to be built on trust.

"You were engaged that night?"

He cringed at the shrill pitch of her voice. He would rather be facing a band of bloodthirsty Celts than Emily at this moment. "I was engaged, Em. 'Was' being the significant word."

"I have a vague memory of asking you if you were married. You told me no."

"I didn't lie. I wasn't married, nor have I ever been married." He remembered trying to hold a normal conversation with Emily as they'd walked from the lobby to the lounge. Once he'd had her in his arms on the dance floor, though, conversation had been the last thing on either of their minds.

Emily's fingers gripped the edge of the table so hard her knuckles turned white. "You just conveniently forgot about this . . ." She waved her hand in the air as if she expected to pluck the words from the room. ". . . this Georgia person."

"In actuality, yes. From the moment I saw you standing in the lobby, Georgia never once entered my mind. The first thought of her hit me while taking my shower the next morning. I knew then that I had to break the engagement."

"So, it took you a whole week to do it?"

He should have known she would pick up on that one. He wasn't sure if she was now upset because he had been engaged or because it had taken him an entire week to break it off. "Georgia was in Virginia attending a couple of auctions at the time, and I didn't think this was something to relay over the phone. Besides, I had other things on my mind."

"Such as?"

Emily appeared to be out for a pound of flesh. He would gladly give it to her if they could put this subject behind them. "I was too busy trying to locate the woman of my dreams, who had disappeared from my bed without leaving a forwarding address. You'd be surprised how few Emilys are listed in the phone book."

"Oh." Emily appeared to think about that for a moment. "That reminds me, how exactly did you find me?"

"I hired a private detective." He was so thankful that she seemed to have calmed down about Georgia, he would gladly tell her anything. "We didn't do a lot of talking that night. The only solid clue I had was that you had mentioned having a sister who worked as a nurse in the ICU at Lancaster General."

"You hired a detective to find me?" Emily was in shock. It was the only word she could think of that described the incredible light feeling she was experiencing. It was either shock or she was about to faint. Adam had actually hired a detective to find her! It was unbelievable. She should be furious that he'd paid someone to poke around in her and her sister's lives. Wasn't that an invasion of privacy?

So why was she feeling so damned flattered?

"I would have done a lot more than that," he said, "if I had only known what. The detective advised me against advertising on billboards for you to call me. He assured me I would get nothing but crank calls. I won't even tell you his reaction to my staking out playgrounds in the hope that you would show up with your kids."

She chuckled at the absurdity of it all. "You're kidding, right?" The billboard number would have had him hauled away by the men in white coats, but staking out playgrounds would have had him locked away by the men in blue.

"Wrong." He reached out and captured her hands, then scooted his chair close to hers. Their knees bumped, jerked away from each other, then bumped once more. "I would have tried anything to find you, Emily. I was desperate."

She could read the honesty in his gaze. Adam meant every word he was saying. He had been searching for her since she'd run from the hotel room. It was a sobering thought. A troubling, romantic thought. A delicious thought that she wanted to wrap around herself for those long, cold winter nights ahead. It was the most romantic thing anyone had ever done for her. She squeezed his hands and smiled. "Thank you."

"For what? Being desperate?"

"No, for not acting like it was a one-night stand." Those three words, "one-night stand," had been haunting her since she'd driven away from the hotel. Her actions had horrified her, embarrassed her, and above all confused her. She wasn't the type of woman who had one-night stands, and she had been appalled knowing that Adam must have thought she was so damn wanton.

"It wasn't a one-night stand, Em," he said seriously.

"What was it, then?" A case of lust at first sight? Insanity? They all boiled down to the same thing. She tried to pull her hands from his grasp.

"It was a beginning." He leaned forward, gripping her hands tighter. "I'm not very good with flowery words, Em. I told you I never believed in passion until I met you. Lust is so simple; it's satisfying your own needs. But passion gets its strength from satisfying someone else's needs."

"Are you trying to say you want to go to bed with me?"

His smile was blinding. "More than I want to breathe, but I'm not asking, at least not now." He released her hands and tenderly stroked her cheek. "You have other needs besides the physical ones, Em. I see your needs in Jordon's wish for a dad, in Samantha's tendency to get dirty by just breathing and the way she clings to her doll, and by the feel of Christopher's small hand nestled in mine."

She felt the tears gather in her eyes and was powerless to stop them. Adam understood. She didn't know how, but he did. She never would have guessed that a man without any children of his own could understand her need to protect, to love, and to cherish her children. Her voice was so low, it didn't even qualify as a whisper as she said, "Thank you." She closed her eyes and pressed her cheek to his warm palm.

"To be perfectly honest with you, Em, I'm scared."

Her eyes flew open at his words. Had she misunderstood the depth of his understanding? "About what?" He looked so intense, she started getting scared herself.

"Everything." He dropped his hand back onto his lap. "You, us, the kids. Take your pick, it doesn't matter."

"I think it matters very much. What scares you?" She already knew what she was afraid of: Adam, a relationship with a man, the effects it would have on the children. Amazingly, they both might be afraid of the same things.

He gave her a small smile and told her the obvious. "I know nothing about children. I've never been around them, and quite frankly, I've never had a desire to have any. Children just weren't on my list of things I wanted out of life."

Her heart sank, and she stopped listening. Adam didn't want children! All her fanciful wishes and dreams had been for nothing. Adam wasn't the man for her, after all.

"Did you hear me, Em?"

She blinked. "What?"

"I asked if you heard me."

"Yeah. You said you didn't want children." She supposed thousands, maybe even millions, of people didn't want children. That was fine by her. She wasn't some reformed smoker who fanatically tried to get everyone else to quit. Just because she was a mother, it didn't mean she wanted to see every other woman with ovaries full of eggs and clear Fallopian tubes popping out kids. The simple truth was, some people just shouldn't be parents. It had just been her bad luck to start falling in love with one such person.

"Did you hear the part about how it was scaring the hell out of me to realize that maybe I had been wrong?"

"About having children?" What was he saying? What had she missed?

"Em, pay attention. I'm only going to say it one more time. I said you and your little band of munchkins have started me thinking about all the things I would miss out on if I didn't have children of my own."

Children of my own! Uh-oh. Children of his own was a world of difference from someone else's children. "What kind of things are you talking about?"

"Watching my son play first base in a ball game."

"What about your daughter?"

"What about a daughter?"

"Why can't you be watching your daughter play first base in a ball game?"

Adam chuckled. "I stand corrected. Watching my son or daughter play first base in a ball game, sloppy kisses and sticky fingers, and let's not forget the pets."

"You have to get rid of the couch."

"What couch?"

"Your couch, your *white* couch, back at the condo. Do you have any idea what children would do to that fabric within a month?" She sadly shook her head at his dazed look. "I won't even tell you what a pet would do to it."

He ran his hand through his hair and growled, "See, Em. That's what I mean!"

She blinked at his unexpected outburst. "You don't want to give up the couch?" This was all hypothetical, so why was he getting so bent out of shape?

"I'd give the couch away without a second thought. It wouldn't even faze me, and I *love* that couch." His fingers did another tour of his hair. "That's what's scaring me."

"Oh." She thought maybe she was beginning to see. "You said yourself that you weren't used to being around children. Maybe since spending some time over here with my kids, you've started to realize they weren't as bad as you always imagined." Spending a few hours here and a few hours there didn't qualify, in her book, as earning mileage toward becoming a parent. Suffer through six months of night feedings, having all three come down with chicken pox at the same time, and several bouts of car sickness and you started to rack up some serious points.

"Maybe," Adam said. "But I think your kids are especially nice and well behaved."

She managed not to laugh, gave him a serene look that would have done the Madonna proud, and kept her mouth shut. Now was the time to change the subject before she had to admit her children were no better and, she prayed, no worse than the majority of kids out there. "What is it about me that scares you?"

Adam studied her face for a long time before he answered. "I'm scared I'm going to lose you again and this time no private detective will be able to help. I'm scared you will keep on comparing me to your late husband and never give me a chance to prove to you that all men aren't created the same." He cupped her face in his hands and brushed her mouth with a kiss. "I'm scared you'll hide behind your kids and old hurts and won't let me love you."

She felt herself melt with every word he spoke. Adam was speaking the truth. She had been comparing him to Ray and hiding behind her children. Maybe it was time to knock down those barriers and start facing life head-on.

Adam cared about her or he wouldn't be there. Most men would have left when she asked them to, and not returned to face the possibility of more rejection. Most men would have looked at her three children and faded back into the woodwork. Most men wouldn't bother to try to understand her fears or her needs. Adam had. Adam wasn't like most men.

She reached up and covered his hands with hers. She could feel a trembling, but didn't know if it came from her or him. It didn't matter. "I'm scared too, Adam."

"Tell me your fears, Em, and I'll try to make them go away." He leaned forward and teased the corner of her mouth with his lips until she smiled.

"I'm scared you're going to hurt me the way Ray did by always putting your business first. I'm scared you'll start looking at my children as excess baggage and figure I'm not worth the price." It was her time to lean forward and kiss the frown that was pulling at his mouth. "I'm scared of my children really falling in love with you and then getting hurt because things didn't work out between us." She kissed him again as his frown deepened. "I'm sorry, Adam, but I'm not a 'me' package any longer, I'm an 'us.' "

"I've known you were a package deal from the beginning, Em. I'll be the first one to admit that I really hadn't given your children much of a thought, but I would never classify them as baggage. Extensions of your heart, definitely. Baggage, never." He turned his hands and interlocked his fingers with hers. "I would never intentionally hurt you or your children, Em. I can't tell you where a relationship with me is going to lead you, because I've never traveled down this road before. But I do know one thing."

"What's that?" His brown eyes were filled with truth and wonder. She wanted to fall into their depths and never come up for air.

"I love you."

She was stunned speechless. Not so much from his declaration, but from the answering cry of her own heart. Adam loved her, and she loved him! She knew there were some powerful emotions twisting and pulling between them, but she hadn't allowed herself to dream of the possibility of love. She was mature enough to know that love and happily-ever-after didn't necessarily go hand in hand. But still . . .

"What, no comment?" he asked.

"A thousand of them are flooding my mind, but I'm not quite sure which one to say." She wanted to ease the vulnerability she saw in his eyes by telling him she returned his love, but she couldn't get the words past her throat. They were scary words. Words that left her wide open for pain. She was having a hard time admitting to herself that she loved Adam, how could she admit it to him? Maybe that was what had been scaring her all along—that she would fall in love with him. Maybe she wasn't so much horrified by what she had done with Adam as by what she had felt toward him.

He gave her a look that was full of compassion and understanding. "It's a frightening thought, isn't it?"

"What?" He couldn't possibly know what she had been thinking.

"Love."

Okay, maybe he had known.

"I think what we need to do, Em, is take it nice and slow. I don't want to rush you into anything you don't feel you're ready for, but I don't what to slink around after dark when the kids are in bed. Since the kids are, and always will be, a very important part of your life, I think they should be involved in whatever kind of relationship we have. Of course, the final decision is yours, but I don't think it would be healthy for you or the kids if you hide the fact that you are a very desirable woman."

"You want my children to see me as *desirable?*" She almost laughed, but held her mirth in. Adam seemed so sincere. He wanted a relationship with her, and he wanted her children involved. Either the man was every single mother's fantasy or he was a glutton for punishment.

"No," he said. "Your children should know you are not only a mother but a woman too."

He had a point there. She had been giving the subject of her dating some serious thought the past couple of days. Longer than that, if she was being honest with herself. The nagging questions had started right after she met Adam.

How was Samantha, when she got older—much, much older—going to form a normal loving relationship with a man when her own mother shied away from every interested male? How were her sons going to handle love? Then there was the question of her children starting to live their own lives. She knew they were too young now, but sooner than she would like, they would all be heading out the door and traveling down paths that would lead them from home. Would they be able to make the journey without feeling guilty for leaving her behind, when all she had in her life was them and a ramshackle old house? Was she causing them more harm than good trying to protect them? Trying to protect herself?

Adam had the insight to understand her dilemma, and he wasn't even a father. Any child would be blessed to have him for a father or, the nagging little voice that refused to be quiet whispered, a stepfather. She wanted a relationship with Adam. She wanted to travel beside him down that road. There was always a chance that it wouldn't work out and she would end up being hurt. It was a fact of life. It hadn't been working out with Ray too well either, and she had been married to him. But she would never know if she rejected Adam's love and asked him to leave.

Some things in life were worth taking that chance. Adam's love was one of those things.

She gave him a look that she prayed was seductive. "Ask me again."

"Ask you what?"

"If I want to make love with you." Once the words were out, she realized the rightness of them. Adam loved her. She loved Adam. They appeared to be destined to be lovers again. The first time she had made love with Adam, she had been in a daze. It had happened so fast, she hadn't even had time to think. Now, when she made love with Adam, it would be with both her body and her mind.

Adam stilled. The only thing on him she could see moving were his eyes. They seemed to search her face for some sign. She smiled and hoped she didn't look as nervous as she felt. "That is, unless you don't want to any longer?"

He quickly found his voice. "Where in the world would you get that idea?"

She shrugged and ducked her head, trying to hide the blush that she could feel sweeping its way up her face. "You seem a little hesitant."

"I'm still trying to decide if I fell asleep in your kitchen and I'm dreaming, or if there really is a fairy godmother who grants wishes." He reached out and tilted her chin up so that she had to look him in the eye. "Would you like to make love with me, Em?"

She felt her stomach clench with desire. Her mouth went dry and her fingers trembled. A million thoughts bombarded her mind. Had she shaved her legs last night, or was it the night before? Why hadn't she put perfume on before Adam showed up? Which pair of panties and bra was she wearing? Please don't let it be the plain white cotton ones she often wore because they were comfortable. She had to run her tongue over her lips before she could speak. "Definitely."

"When?"

Oh Lord, what was he doing, playing twenty questions? What had happened to the spontaneity of that first night? "Now, and before you ask where, I have a perfectly good queen-size bed upstairs and a door that locks. The only thing I have to do is bring Wellington in and lock up for the night." She stood and walked to the patio door. "So if you are staying, stay. If not . . ." She didn't know how to finish that statement, so she opened the door and clapped her hands loudly.

Adam walked up behind her as Wellington slowly got to his feet, stretched, and padded his way into the kitchen. Adam waited until she had closed the glass door and clicked the lock, then he turned her around and brushed back a curl that had escaped her French braid. "Are you nervous, Em? I thought we pretty much killed any first-time jitters between us."

"This is the first time my head's involved, Adam. I keep thinking that somehow it isn't going to live up to my memories of that first night."

"Funny, I keep thinking it's going to be better." He brushed her mouth with a gentle kiss.

Emily leaned into his warmth and allowed the sweet kiss to calm her fears. What did she have to worry about? Adam had seen everything there was to see—the faded stretch marks on her breasts and the tops of her thighs; the soft stomach that refused to tighten any further, no matter how many sit-ups and stomach crunches she did—and still Adam had found her desirable enough to come back.

She pulled away from him and smiled. "Are you up to sneaking past three sleeping kids?"

He grinned. "I'm up for a lot of things, Em. What do you have in mind?"

She chuckled as she glanced around the kitchen. It looked fine to her. Whatever was left out, was left out. She headed for the hallway, turning the kitchen light off as she went.

Adam followed silently along behind her as she turned off the living room and front porch lights and locked the door. Silently they climbed the stairs. Neither one touched the other. It was as if they both knew that with one touch, the control would be gone. They would never make it to the safety of her bedroom.

Emily resisted the urge to check on the children one more time. She knew they were safe and asleep, but old habits were hard to break. She and Adam stepped into her room, and she closed and locked the door behind them.

The click of the lock was still echoing in the room when Adam hauled her into his arms and kissed her the way she had been dreaming about. Hot, hard, and so thoroughly that only her dentist had a more intimate knowledge of her mouth.

She should have known it was going to be this explosive between them. Hadn't she lived through the explosion once before? His mouth made heated demands she was more than willing to fulfill. Her hands stroked his back and toyed with his soft dark hair as she pressed herself closer. Her body remembered the feel of him and trembled with anticipation.

She bit his lip and moaned as his hands captured her breasts and lightly squeezed. Her nipples hardened and beaded beneath the layers of clothes that separated them. Suddenly the trappings of civilization were too much. She wanted to feel the warmth of his skin beneath her hands, the roughness of the hair that covered his thighs as they brushed against hers, and the length of him as he surged inside her. All of him. She wanted Adam to make the ache go away.

As she pulled his shirt from the waistband of his pants and tugged it upward, she felt the zipper of her dress come undone. Their kiss broke for barely a second as his shirt was yanked over his head and her dress pooled at her feet. Emily stepped out of her sandals as she kicked the dress out of the way.

Adam's hands captured hers when she reached for his belt buckle. "We have to slow down, Em." He sounded as if he had just run the Boston Marathon—and won.

She placed a kiss on his collarbone and started to work her way down his chest. "This is slow, Adam. You should see me when I'm in a hurry."

He chuckled, but kept hold of her hands as he stepped back toward the bed. "Behave yourself." He reached for the comforter and yanked it down.

Emily teased with her tongue a nipple that had pushed itself out of the dark curls that covered his chest. "You won't be saying that in two minutes."

He groaned as he unsnapped her bra and peeled it down her arms. He got his revenge by turning the tables on her and pulling one of her jutting nipples deep into his mouth. If he hadn't been holding her, she would have crumbled to the floor.

Her hips arched into his, and she could feel his arousal, thick and heavy behind the barrier of his zipper. Adam anchored her hips against his and shuddered.

Within a heartbeat she was stripped of her last barrier, a pair of green satin and lace panties, and swept up into Adam's arms. She ran her tongue over the pulse thundering away beneath the tanned skin of his neck. He smelled like expensive cologne and tasted like Adam. That taste had been haunting her dreams for weeks.

He laid her in the center of her bed, and she watched with rapt attention as he kicked off his shoes and stripped off his pants. He was beautiful in his masculinity. Narrow hips and wide shoulders that were usually covered with the expensive business suits, shirts, and ties were now bared for her gaze. For her touch. She reached out a hand, and he lowered himself onto the bed, pulling her into his arms.

Skin against skin. Mouths and hands seeking, finding. The heat they generated ignited a fuse, and she could feel the desire build to an explosion. There could be only one conclusion to the rapidly escalating fervor, and she wanted it now. There would be time later for a more exploratory, leisurely pace. But right this minute she needed Adam more than she had ever needed anything before.

Emily wrapped her hand around his straining arousal and guided him home. She felt the control he was trying to maintain as he slowly slid into her heat. She didn't want control. She wanted wildness. Her thighs squeezed his hips as she arched against him, pulling him in deeper. His name was a plea as it tumbled from her lips.

Adam's control shattered as she matched him thrust for thrust. Always increasing, always closer to the peak. The explosion was coming, and they were both going to shatter. Emily was determined that Adam was going to be with her as she climaxed. She held on until she saw the blaze in his eyes turn wild. Her arms pulled him closer and she wrapped her legs around the back of his thighs. "Now, Adam, now!"

She felt his release coincide with her own. Her name was torn from his throat as the explosion took them both.

Twenty minutes later Emily lay in Adam's arms and marveled at the strength of two people who could survive such an eruption. Under her cheek she could hear that Adam's heart had calmed and was now thudding away at its normal rate. Her fingers toyed with a batch of curls circling his nipple. A light summer breeze was stirring the curtains, but it wasn't strong enough to chill them. The comforter and top sheet were still lying on the floor where they had been shoved earlier.

Adam stirred slightly and she smiled. Good, he wasn't asleep. Her fingers inched down his chest as her big toe teased its way up his calf. She wanted to play this time. The initial heat had erupted; now she wanted to build the fire slowly. Her hand slid lower.

Marcia Evanick174

Adam sucked in a shocked breath and captured her wandering fingers before they reached their goal. "Emily, what do you think you're doing?"

She smiled against his chest and teased a protruding nipple with her tongue. He hadn't sounded upset at her curious touch. His voice had contained desire with a touch of laughter. "I'm thanking you for the roses." She tugged her hand out of his and gently cupped his growing arousal. Her breath feathered his chest. "Have any objections?"

He hauled her up onto his chest. His mouth was touching hers when he whispered, "Not a one."

It was the last coherent word either said for a very long time.

TEN

Adam closed the car door behind him as he glanced at the broken wheel of the baby stroller, then at Samantha's tear-streaked face as she stood next to the driveway. Soft green eyes, so much like Emily's, were filled with more tears. One after another they rolled down her cheeks and gripped his heart.

"Please, please, please, Adam, can you fix it?" Samantha clutched her doll to her chest and gave a small, watery hiccup. "Holly wants to go for her walk."

He squatted by the pink plastic stroller and examined the little hard-rubber wheel. The cotter pin had worked its way out and was now missing somewhere in the grass. It would be a simple enough job to repair the wheel, once he found another cotter pin or a reasonable substitute. He would either fix the doll stroller or go buy her a new one. Her tears were ripping his heart to shreds.

How could one little girl become so important to

him so quickly? Jordon, Samantha, and Christopher had braided themselves into a single loving strand and wrapped their way around his heart. They were now an intricate part of his feelings toward Emily, feelings that had grown ever stronger in the past several weeks.

"Tell Holly to hold her diaper on," he said. "I'll have this fixed in a jiffy." He opened his arms, and Samantha plowed into his chest with the force of a small tornado—a small, dirty tornado—nearly throwing him off balance.

He didn't even cringe when she buried her face into his clean shirt and cried, "Can you really fix it now?"

"Sure, sweetheart." A moist kiss landed on his cheek, and he silently vowed he would either fix the wheel or die trying. "Why don't you run into the house and tell your mom I have some important business to take care of before I toss those steaks onto the grill."

When he had called Emily that afternoon from work, she had promised him potato salad, corn on the cob, and fresh squeezed lemonade if he cooked the steaks she had bought on the backyard grill. It sounded like paradise to him, so he'd left work at exactly five o'clock, prompting his secretary to question his health. After he'd assured her he had never felt better, he had driven to his condo to shower and change into something relaxing and cool. If he could change one thing about Emily's house besides the hideous color, he would make sure it had central air-conditioning, especially in the bedroom.

He watched as Sam ran toward the house, blond ponytail swishing across her back. The tears had stopped and he had been elevated in her eyes to the Fix-It God. He chuckled as he picked up the wheel and the stroller and headed for Emily's garage. He hadn't the faintest notion why Emily called it a garage. She couldn't fit even the front fender of her minivan into the overcrowded, jam-packed, filled-to-the-rafters building that on good days appeared to be leaning toward the left.

He had had his first glimpse of the "garage" the week before, when he had helped Emily work on her dining room. First they had stripped the rooster wallpaper off the walls, then decided to rip up the mud-colored carpeting. He had come out to the garage in search of some tools to help with the carpet. What he had found were tools ranging from a newly purchased circular saw to a plane that belonged in some hardware museum. Emily not only had Ray's he-man collection of what the modern garage should contain—and most of those tools were still in their original boxes—but she still had her grandfather's collection. Some of the tools might even predate her grandfather. In fact, they looked as if they'd been used to build the house she was living in.

Adam pulled the garage doors open and steadied Jordon's new bike as it threatened to fall into the driveway. He squeezed past two other bikes, stepped over a wagon and a sled, and moved a snow shovel out of his way. The lawn mower Emily used was by the front, but there were two others, including one of those wicked looking push jobs, barring the way to the workbench. He remembered seeing row after row of baby food jars filled with nuts, bolts, nails, and everything in between. Somewhere in that nightmarish clutter had to be a cotter pin.

He held the stroller over his head and slowly maneuvered his way toward the back. A leaf rake tried to attack his ankle, and he bruised his shin on the handle of what appeared to be the first wringer washing machine ever made.

He placed the stroller and wheel on top of a stack of wooden crates and started his search. Light filtered through the dust-coated multipaned window overlooking the workbench. He was rewarded within minutes by finding a cotter pin. Only problem was, it was large enough to hold on the wheel of a locomotive.

He was cursing under his breath, trying to remove the top of one of the baby food jars that looked promising, when Emily's voice reached him. "Adam?"

"Back here, Em. Don't come in, it's too dangerous." The top finally budged and the assorted cotter pins that hadn't felt air from this century gleamed up at him. "Bingo!"

"What did you say?"

He turned toward the door and smiled at Emily. She had Christopher perched on one hip, and Sam was holding one of her hands. She looked hot, tired, and incredibly lovely. "I said, you really should give some thought to cleaning out this place." He selected a small pin and placed the jar in the only clear space on the table.

"I have given it some thought, but every time I open the door I change my mind."

He chuckled as he set the wheel back on the stroller and tapped the cotter pin on with a monkey wrench he had found nearby. "I can see your point." He gave the wheel a turn. It spun freely. He had fixed the stroller. "Hey, Sam?"

"Did you fix it?" Sam shouted as she tried to peer over the fortress of obstacles.

"Tell Holly to get her walking dress on. It's time to go for a stroll." He replaced the lid on the jar and put it back where he'd found it. No telling when future generations of Pierces would need a cotter pin. He lifted the stroller up over his head again and started to make his way out. This time he avoided the leaf rake and washing machine, but he didn't see the fireplace poker until it jabbed him in the side. "Ouch!"

"Are you all right?" Emily exclaimed, standing on her toes to get a better view of him.

"Don't worry Em, it's nothing seven stitches won't close."

"Adam!"

He heard the alarm in her voice and quickly reassured her. "I was only joking." He knew there might be a red mark on his side, but there surely wasn't any blood. "I really think you should clean this place out. The Smithsonian might be interested in half the stuff in here." He maneuvered himself out of the garage and lowered the stroller to the driveway. He brushed Emily's mouth with a welcoming kiss before ruffling

Christopher's hair. "If Christopher ever got in there, we'd never find him."

Sam immediately strapped in Holly and started to push her toward the backyard. "Thank you, Adam."

"You're welcome, sweet thing." He waved at the little doll. "You too, Holly." Sam's laughter followed her.

Christopher reached out to him, and Adam effortlessly plucked him from his mother's arms. "Hey, sport, have you been behaving yourself today?"

"Today, pooh!" answered the boy.

"Yeah." Adam grinned. "I have days like that too."

Emily playfully whacked Adam in the side. "He's trying to tell you today we washed Winnie-the-Pooh and his blanket and they're hanging on the line drying."

"Whoa. Bath day for Pooh. Big things happening at the Pierce house." He swung the boy up onto his shoulders, where he knew Christopher was hoping to be. He gave the boy a playful bounce. "Did you get behind his ears?"

"Ears!" shouted Christopher as he grabbed Adam's and used them for handles.

Adam knew he had only himself to blame for that blunder. He gave another bounce and grinned at Emily as Christopher squealed with delight. "Miss me?" He wanted to kiss her again, this time more properly, but she was still uncomfortable showing any signs of affection around the kids. A quick kiss now and then was all she allowed. But it was more than what she had allowed two weeks earlier.

She surprised him by stepping in front of him and staring at his mouth, seemingly engrossed by it. After glancing at Christopher, who was busily reaching for the leaves above his head, she leaned forward and captured his mouth in a world-record-setting pace of a kiss.

If he hadn't been holding on to Christopher, he would have hauled her into his arms and lengthened that kiss until next Tuesday. He grinned instead. It was the first kiss she had ever initiated in front of the kids. The steps their relationship were taking were small, but they were all heading in the right direction. "You *really* must have missed me," he said.

"It's only been twelve hours."

"Counting the hours, Em?"

"If I were, it would be more like thirteen. Someone left at five o'clock this morning instead of his usual six."

"You did miss me!" He gave her another quick kiss. "It was business." He could see the curiosity in her gaze, not condemnation. He had been walking such a fine tightrope between Emily and his business, half the time he didn't know which way to lean. His early morning routine of sneaking out of the house before the kids woke up had been working so far, but that morning he had needed to arrive earlier at the office to deal with some sorely neglected work.

His business wasn't suffering yet from his shortened hours. But the key word was "yet." He knew he couldn't continue to walk this tightrope without risk. On one side was everything he had ever worked for. It was his identity, who he was. Adam Benjamin Young, architect. On the other side was his heart, where Emily and her band of merry munchkins had taken up residence. He couldn't afford to lose either half of himself, but he hadn't yet found the perfect combination that would allow him to have it all.

Emily was still jittery every time he mentioned his business. It was as if she expected him to start putting in twenty-hour days and ignoring her and the kids. She still sounded surprised whenever he called during the day just to say hi, or to see what was on her schedule for that evening.

There were a lot of unresolved issues between Emily and himself, but the most glaring was the fact that not once had she told him how she felt. No words of love had passed her lips. There had been words of playful affection, even some serious tones occasionally, and definitely words of desire. But never words of love. He needed those words. He needed to know that Emily returned his love and that there was hope for a future. A future together. Somehow they had to get past her fear of his business while satisfying his need to succeed. It was a troubling situation, but one he hadn't even begun to give up on.

Adam jostled and bounced Christopher across the yard and onto the back patio. The picnic table had already been draped with a red-and-white-checkered cloth, and a tray containing five dinner plates, two glasses, and three cups was sitting on one end. Samantha was pushing Holly in circles around Wellington, who was lying in the center of the patio chewing on what appeared to be the biggest bone Adam had ever seen outside a museum.

He swung Christopher off his shoulders and stood him on the patio. Nodding toward the dog, he said to Emily, "I see Wellington caught himself a *Tyrannosaurus rex* this afternoon."

Emily grinned at Wellington. He had been in doggie heaven for hours with his present. "My sister stopped by for lunch and a visit before she was due in for her shift."

Adam raised his eyebrows. "Remind me never to check in to that hospital."

"Relax. Charmaine is dating a butcher."

Adam shuddered. "Like I said, remind me never to check in to that hospital."

Emily chuckled. Adam's sense of humor was a continued delight. "Wait here, Mr. Comedian. I'll bring you out the steaks." She dashed into the house, opened the refrigerator, and reached for the plate with the steaks all ready for the grill. She retraced her steps and handed Adam the plate. "You start on these while I go finish up the rest of the stuff."

She returned to the kitchen and carefully dropped the dozen ears of corn into the pot of boiling water while listening to her children talk to Adam. Or to be more accurate, Adam talk to her children.

There were so many sides to Adam, each and every one of them an intriguing piece of the puzzle that made up the whole. She had seen a lot of those puzzle pieces, except for the one she needed to see the most, the businessman.

So far he had managed to separate that side of his life from her, but for how much longer? She knew why he did it; it was her fear. He was trying to protect her from the reality of his life. Adam hadn't achieved all he had done by putting in eight-hour days and leaving the office behind at five o'clock. Every night for the past two weeks he had spent with her and the children. Last Saturday he had treated them to a day at Dutch Wonderland and dinner at one of the famous Pennsylvania Dutch restaurants. It had been a fun family day, but that night behind her bedroom door had been magical.

Adam had given her back the magic of love. He had given her back hope. It had been from that night on that she had really started to believe that a future with him was possible. The children had surrendered to his charms without a struggle. They would accept him with open arms.

Maybe all of her fears were groundless. Adam had never once treated her or the children as second-class anything. But since he wasn't giving her the true picture of how he normally lived his life, how involved he was in his business, it was hard to make a final judgment. If she could ever make a final judgment. People changed all the time. Ray hadn't been a workaholic when she'd married him. Who was to say if she married a workaholic, he wouldn't turn into an unemployed couch potato?

She glanced out the kitchen window and watched as Adam flipped a steak and teased Christopher about something. Christopher pointed to Pooh and his ratty-edged blanket which were both still hanging on the clothesline in the late afternoon sun. Adam closed the lid of the grill and went to unpin Pooh, who was hanging by his ears, and handed the bear to her son. She felt her heart lighten as Christopher rewarded Adam with a big kiss that landed somewhere in the vicinity of his chin.

Just then Jordon came into view from around the side of the house. Coming home, he must have heard the commotion in the backyard and headed there instead of the house. Jordon greeted Adam and immediately went into a conversation about baseball. Adam kept the discussion going as he opened the lid to the grill and checked the steaks.

No, the kids would have no problems accepting Adam into their lives. Half the time, Jordon acted like he was the savior of the family because he'd wished up Adam in the first place. If only life were so simple.

"Hey, Emily," Adam called. "Are you about ready for these beauties? If I cook them any longer, they're going to taste like the soles of Jordon's sneakers!"

"Dish them up, Young." She chuckled as Jordon made an appropriate sound to how appetizing that sounded. "It's coming, it's coming."

Later that night a very satisfied Emily snuggled deeper into Adam's embrace. How could making love with Adam get any better? Night after night she had been expecting not exactly boredom, but something akin to normalcy. Night after night Adam had showed her just how wrong she was. Tonight had been no exception.

The kids had been asleep in their beds for quite a while when Adam had surprised her by joining her in the shower. She'd been immediately thankful for the upstairs renovations she had done the month after she had moved into the house. The newly constructed master bedroom's walk-in closet separated the equally new master bath from the rest of the house. She had never had so much fun with a simple bar of soap and water in her life.

As Emily lay there, she realized she didn't want to wake up alone tomorrow morning, or any other morning. She wanted to playfully tease Adam awake before the kids got up and commanded her attention. She wanted to pick out his tie to match his suit and shirt. She wanted to share her first cup of coffee with someone besides Wellington and two arrogant cats. She wanted to cook Adam breakfast, send him off to work with a kiss, and know he'd be home for dinner.

"Adam, are you up?"

The warm palm of his hand stroked her thigh and hip with suggestive intent. "Lord, woman, are you trying to kill me?"

She smiled. He didn't sound too upset with the prospects of going for round two, even if that hadn't been what was on her mind. "Relax, Adam. Your body is safe with me. I just want to talk."

His hand caressed her bottom and gave it a light squeeze. "Don't let it be said that I'm a spoilsport. I'm more than willing to *up*hold my end."

She could feel his growing desire nudging her thigh and knew exactly what was *up*. The room was in almost total darkness, with only a faint glow from the streetlight filtering through the curtains. The darkness didn't bother her. She liked lying in the dark with Adam. Many a night she had just lain there pretending they were married and he wouldn't be sneaking off before the kids woke up. Maybe it was time to stop pretending.

"Adam, tell me about your work."

She felt him stiffen beneath her. "What do you want to know?"

"Eventually, everything. But start with something simple. Like, who was your first employee? What was the first building you designed? What's your favorite building that you designed? Did you ever have any really strange request when designing a house, like mirrored ceilings or secret passageways?"

He relaxed and chuckled. "Mirrored ceilings, hmmm . . . Let me see . . ."

She captured his wandering hand and interlocked her fingers with his, holding the hand in place. "Behave, Adam. I seriously want to know about your firm. I'm also curious as to how it's surviving without you at its helm."

"What do you mean without me? I'm there every day."

"I'm not talking about Monday through Friday eight till five, Adam. I want to know what kind of hours you used to put in before you met me. My money's on twelve-hour days and six-day weeks."

"Em, that's an unfair question. Before I met you, I had nothing to come home to."

"What about Georgia? You were an engaged man. Surely she must have meant something to you."

"Of course she meant something to me, Em. But comparing what I feel toward you and what I felt toward Georgia would be like comparing a Frank Lloyd Wright design with *Better Homes and Gardens'* house plan number 101. There's just no comparison."

"So what you're saying is that I was right when I guessed twelve-hour days, six days a week?"

"No! I mean, yes! Oh hell, Em. That's not fair."

She nibbled on her bottom lip for a moment. Adam was right, it wasn't fair to compare how much time he had spent on his business before he met her to now. It would be like comparing how much time and attention she had given the kids before Adam had entered her life and now. Adam had taken a large chunk of her attention and time, but it didn't mean the kids were suffering or that she loved them any less. It meant she had made room in her busy life for Adam. Maybe he had done the same for her and her children.

"You're right, Adam, that wasn't fair." She pressed a kiss over his thudding heart and felt him relax. "I want to understand this other love you have. Do you think the kids and I could visit your office some day when you're not too busy?"

"Are you serious, Em?"

"Of course I'm serious." She leaned up on her elbow and tried to see his face. It was too dark. "I'm truly interested in what you do."

"Tomorrow. Come tomorrow around eleven and I'll treat you all to lunch."

Tomorrow! Was he crazy? She couldn't interrupt his schedule like that. "I don't want to impose on you, Adam. Just let me know when you might have a few free minutes and we'll stop by then."

He hauled her back into his arms and gave her a hug that threatened to crack a rib or two. "Tomorrow, Em. I expect all four of you to be there at eleven o'clock or I'll come looking for you."

ELEVEN

Emily glanced in awe around the reception area of Young Architects and Design. She gripped Christopher's hand tighter and prayed that Samantha and Jordon didn't touch a thing. There were no plastic chairs or vinyl-coated couches in sight. The antique furniture that blended perfectly with the elegance of the sweeping foyer was either the real McCoy or expensive reproductions. If she had been a rich client looking for an architect to design her home or building, she would have hired Adam's firm on the basis of this foyer alone.

The receptionist gave Emily a friendly smile as she hung up the phone. "Mr. Young will be right down."

Emily nervously returned the smile. "Thank you." The young receptionist looked poised and highly capable. She also looked at Emily and the children with a great deal of curiosity.

When she had first stepped into the building and

told the receptionist she was there to see Mr. Young, the woman had informed her that Mr. Young was expecting her and the children. She had been flattered that Adam had taken the time to tell the receptionist that he was expecting her. But now she wondered what else Adam might have told her. By the covert glances the woman was shooting her and the children, she would have to guess Adam didn't receive a lot of female visitors. Especially females with three children in tow.

"Adam!" Samantha shouted as she spotted Adam coming down the stairs.

Emily cringed as Samantha ran across the room to meet him. Jordon was right on her heels and Christopher tugged on her hand so hard that she had to release the boy. What was one more child in the melee? She was already embarrassed beyond belief. Adam was never going to forgive her for disrupting his business. They had been invited for a quick tour, not a shouting match. Christopher's yell was still echoing off the walls.

On the rare occasions when Ray had allowed her to bring the children to his office, he would become irate if there was so much as a peep from one of them. It had taken her a couple of visits to realize Ray hadn't invited her or the kids because he missed them, he had done it to show off his perfect little family to the employees. She rarely visited his offices in center city after that.

She waited with dread for Adam's reaction to the kids' enthusiastic greeting. Any second now she was going to see Adam in the role of businessman, not lover. She wasn't sure she was ready for the switch, but that was why she'd asked to come in the first place. She needed to see the other side of Adam.

A moment later her mouth fell open in shock as Adam gave Samantha a quick hug, ruffled Jordon's neatly combed hair, and swung Christopher up into his arms. He was grinning at the kids and at her! He didn't appear mad, upset, or the least bit put out by the children's boisterous greeting. In fact, he looked damn happy to see them.

When was she going to expect a certain reaction out of Adam and actually get it? The quiet voice inside her was no longer little. It was loud and blaring. *Maybe when you stop comparing him to Ray!* Her inner voice was right. She was still unjustly comparing Adam to Ray. It was about time she stopped.

She answered Adam's grin with one of her own as he walked toward her. He was still carrying Christopher and holding Sam's hand. Jordon was one step to his left. "Hi, are you sure you're up to this?" she asked.

He gave her a quick kiss. "Been waiting all morning to give you the tour." He glanced at the receptionist, who was smiling at them all. "We might as well start here. Emily, I would like you to meet Shelia Peatman. Shelia's been our receptionist for years. We wouldn't know what to do without her."

He tugged Emily closer to the desk. "Shelia, I'd like you to meet Emily Pierce and her children, Jordon, Samantha, and"—he bounced the boy in his arms—"Christopher."

And so the tour began. For the next thirty minutes Emily and the kids were shown huge copying machines that copied monster-size blueprints, offices on every floor, and nearly two dozen people whose names she didn't even try to memorize. The kids stole the entire show. Everyone was polite and cordial to her, but as soon as they saw her children, the rules changed. Secret stashes of M&M's were ripped open, flying toasters appeared on computer screens, and one designer did a quick sketch of Winnie-the-Pooh for Christopher.

She had to stop at the "little girls' room" with Samantha, and when they returned she found Adam and two other architects hunched around a computer, showing Jordon how to design his own house with what appeared to be a computerized set of architectural Colorforms. Christopher was holding court with another handful of employees. He was sitting in the middle of the hall coloring on a blueprint that was nearly three times his size.

They finally ended the tour in Adam's office. Well, she and Adam were in his office. The kids were outside the door being spoiled by his secretary, a nice grandmotherly type who obviously loved children.

Adam leaned against his desk and asked, "So, what do you think?"

She glanced at some rough sketches scattered across a huge table standing against one wall. They were quick pencil drawings of a house Adam must have been working on earlier. She walked over to the desk and stopped directly in front of him. "I'm impressed both by the business and"—she moved in closer and nudged her way to stand between his legs—"by the man who runs it."

He looked so darn cool and collected in his dark gray suit and designer tie. Not a hair was out of place. She wondered exactly how calm he really was beneath that starched shirt. She had agonized over what to wear herself, what to dress the kids in, and even if she should come. She had had on three different outfits before finally selecting on a flowing flower print skirt and a simple, but silk, top.

Adam had no right to look so darn confident when she was jumping at every little noise. As her sister had told her the day before at lunch, when Emily had confided her worries about Adam and their relationship, there was nothing wrong with her except that she was a little gun-shy. Charmaine's advice had been to pick up the gun and pull the trigger herself. She should stop waiting for Adam to make the next move, then jump when he did. If you're the one holding the gun and squeezing the trigger, Charmaine had said, the loud bang doesn't startle you as much.

It sounded like wonderful advice for a gunslinger or a cowboy, but Emily wasn't sure how it would hold up against Adam. Still, she was willing to give it a try, and right now seemed like a perfect opportunity.

Her skirt flowed around his thighs as she leaned in closer and playfully nipped at his lower lip. She was rewarded by his low groan and his hands gripping her hips and pulling her in tighter. His suit had cost more than what she budgeted for food for an entire month, but it couldn't conceal his desire. She smiled and deepened the kiss.

Heat erupted as lips clung and tongues searched. Adam's hands cupped her bottom and brought her firmly against his growing arousal. Emily arched her back, pressing his fullness against her emptiness. Her trembling fingers wove through his hair as she surrendered to the passion that was consuming them.

The fact that they were in his office faded away. Nothing mattered but the taste, the feel, and the hunger of Adam. Her children were on the other side of the office door and could walk in at any time, and it still didn't matter. She wanted Adam and she wanted him now.

"Excuse me, Adam." His secretary's voice coming over the intercom forced them apart. "The kids have a message for you and their mother."

"We're hungry!" cried all three children in unison.

Emily buried her face against his chest and groaned. She wasn't sure if she was embarrassed for what could have happened or aggravated that it hadn't. She had never made love in an office before, and the way she had been kissing Adam, she wouldn't have stopped him if he had tried.

He kept one arm wrapped around Emily, holding her close to his chest, as he leaned back and hit the intercom button on his phone. "We hear you. Give us a minute to finish up in here and we'll be right out."

She could hear the desire in his hoarse voice and

prayed the intercom hadn't picked it up. She only had herself to blame for this embarrassing moment. She had been the one to start it. Adam had been acting like the perfect gentleman and tour guide. It was all her sister's fault. Emily never should have listened to that stupid advice about guns. What did Charmaine know about long-term commitments or, for that matter, about a relationship that lasted more than three weeks?

"Em?" Adam cupped her chin and forced her to raise her face.

The passion and concern in his eyes pulled at her heart. He looked just as startled as she felt. She gave him a crooked little smile, pointed an imaginary gun at him, and said, "Bang!"

Adam squeezed Emily's hand and tugged her along. Jordon, Christopher, and Sam were already at the next booth, and he didn't want to lose sight of them. Lititz Park was jam-packed for its annual Fourth of July celebration. Dusk was approaching and soon it would be time to return to their blanket on the grass for the main show: fireworks.

The week since Emily and the kids' tour of his business had been amazing. Emily had been asking one question after another. She had even piled the kids into the minivan and insisted on a driving tour of some of the houses he had designed. He had taken them to Lavender Hall and shown them the beautiful mansion, now that the majority of the renovations had been completed. Emily had been duly impressed. The kids had been more interested in the swimming pool and the riding stables.

He didn't fully understand this turnaround in Emily, but he was indeed grateful for it, and he knew the instant the change had begun. The difference in Emily had started that afternoon in his office when he had nearly made love to her and they had been interrupted by his secretary and the children. He was still perplexed by her action of pointing an imaginary gun and saying "Bang." He had asked her then and later that night, when they had finally found the privacy and time to finish what they had started in his office, but Emily never gave him an answer. She had only smiled a secret womanly smile that had been around since the beginning of time and had probably given the original Adam some serious second thoughts.

Adam hadn't the first clue as to what the gun action had been about, but he loved the end results. Emily was no longer intimidated by the other half of his life. In fact, she had been crossing over the line between his work and his private life so often this past week, he believed she was seeing him at last as a whole man, not the two halves she had neatly separated him into.

"Hey, Mom. Hey, Adam!" shouted Samantha. "Come see this!"

Adam pulled Emily closer as they maneuvered around the crowd. "What do you say, Em? Should we go see what's so important?" His whole life he had lived in Lancaster County, excluding four years away at college, and never once had he been tempted to visit Lititz's Fourth of July celebration. When Emily had told him she'd promised to take the kids, he had been tempted. Not only because that was where Emily and the kids were going to be, but because he had been curious as to what else in life he had been missing out on.

Ever since he'd met Emily and the kids, he'd realized that not only had he been missing out on a whole lot of life, but he'd been missing out on a whole lot of love as well. Emily and her children loved him. He knew that with the same clarity that he knew his name. He just hadn't heard the words yet. He was a patient man. He could wait until Emily was ready. He only prayed that he wouldn't have to wait too much longer.

"It's probably something to buy," Emily said, "and don't you dare get them one more thing. You're spoiling them."

"I am not. I'll have you know that spoiling children goes against my principles." He pulled her in closer as a frazzled elderly couple with two rowdy grandchildren in tow squeezed past them. "Now, spoiling their mother . . ." He kissed the side of her neck. "That's a different story."

Emily ducked her head and blushed wildly. "Don't you dare send me another bouquet of flowers. The neighbors are beginning to talk."

"About us?" He didn't like the idea of anyone talking about Emily because of him.

"No, about me and the young, good-looking man

who delivers those flowers. In the past two weeks he's been to my house seven times!"

"Young? Good-looking?" He pretended outrage, but he could see the laughter lurking in her soft green eyes. The neighbors probably were talking, but it wasn't about the deliveryman. The neighbors had to have seen him arrive at her house every night around dinnertime and leave every morning around six. Hell, the neighbors probably thought he was living there. Realistically speaking, the neighbors were right. "If I had known that, I would have figured out another way of getting those flowers to you."

"You don't have to send me so many flowers, Adam."

He glanced over at the children, who were standing in front of a booth filled with dozens of little fishbowls. For fifty cents you could get ten Ping-Pong balls to toss at the bowls. If a ball landed in a bowl, you won a goldfish. He had a feeling Sam's tank might be receiving some new residents that night.

He winked at the kids and turned back toward Emily. The crowd hustled and bustled around them, but he didn't hear the noise or the laughter. He saw only Emily. "I have to keep sending them, Em."

The laughter in her eyes faded. "Why?"

He grinned. "Because I love the way you thank me for them." He brushed a quick kiss across her mouth before she had a chance to do more than laugh. "Come on, let's go win Sam some playmates for her fishies."

❖———————❖

Emily leaned back against Adam and sighed as the first rocket streaked through the dark sky and burst into a brilliant shower of green sparks. Night had fallen and the show had begun.

The soft blue quilt she had spread on the ground earlier was comfortable, if a little crowded. The grassy area of the park was dotted with more blankets and chairs than green splotches of grass. She had selected an area far enough away from the crushing mass of humanity to offer them a smidgen of privacy. Anything above a whisper would be heard by the couple with the sleeping baby twenty feet away or the lip-locked teenagers directly behind them.

Her kids were at the front edge of the quilt, leaning back on their elbows and staring at the night sky in wonder. Jordon was acting like a sports commentator, giving the younger two a bang-by-bang description of the light show overhead. Christopher was squeezed in between his brother and sister. Behind them sat a stuffed green dog Adam had won for Christopher, three goldfish in separate plastic bags, and a four-foot blow-up baseball bat that Jordon had won by tossing darts at colored circles.

Emily and Adam had the rear edge of the quilt. It wasn't much in the way of privacy, but they were together and it was seductively dark. She leaned farther back and smiled as Adam's hand stroked the curve of her hip. She could hear his strong heartbeat beneath her ear, and the heat of his body warmed her back. He felt solid and safe. He felt like forever.

She watched as a huge gold barrage of sparks illuminated the sky. Oohs and aahs rose from the park in waves. She smiled. She would like to ooh and aah, but it wouldn't be for the showy fireworks celebration. Her awe-inspired appreciation would be for the man behind her. How was it possible to be more in love with him today than she had been last week or even yesterday? Did that mean she would love him more tomorrow? Probably. She couldn't imagine a day going by when she didn't love Adam.

So what was she going to do about it?

Tell him! Ah, the voice of reason has risen once again. She wanted to tell Adam, but she didn't want to do it in the heat of passion. Her love for him was passionate and the desire they shared was a large part of their relationship. But it wasn't the whole relationship. Her love was also safe and comfortable, like now. It included laughter and playfulness, yet there was a serious side to it as well.

His business no longer frightened her. Adam wasn't obsessed the way Ray had been. Adam wasn't anything like her late husband. Adam would know when to put business first over family. She wasn't so naive as to think that Adam would always put her and the children first. There would be occasions when he had to work late or on the weekends. It was part of his life. It was part of who he was, and the love she felt toward him was unconditional.

Just like his love for her. His love would have to be

unconditional to include her children. Taking on someone else's three children was an enormous responsibility, one Adam seemed more than willing and capable of assuming. He'd known she came as a package deal from the very beginning. It was only right, then, that she should declare her love with her little "packages" close by.

She nestled her head against his shoulder and whispered, "Adam?"

He dropped a light kiss along her jaw. "Hmmm . . ." He turned his face back up toward the heavens.

She waited for the tracer of another rocket to speed up into the sky. When it reached its pinnacle, and just before it exploded, she whispered, "I love you."

The park filled with awed exclamations as the majestic purple fireworks exploded into glorious color overhead. Adam's fingers stilled on her hip and his head snapped down to stare at her. "Dammit, Em," he growled.

She bit her lip and continued to watch the sky for the next explosion of color. This holding-the-gun business was hell on the nerves. "I take it you aren't thrilled with that little announcement?" How could she have been that wrong? How could she have misjudged Adam like that?

His lips tickled her ear as he whispered, "It's your timing I'm not thrilled with." He glanced meaningfully at the kids sitting less than four feet away and the crowd scattered about them.

She closed her eyes as a series of white flashes and loud bangs filled the sky. This time she didn't jump at the explosions. After all, she was the one holding the gun. "What's wrong with my timing?" As far as she was concerned, her timing was perfect. If he thought her declaration of love was lousy timing, wait until she squeezed off the second round.

His teeth nipped playfully at her ear. All she had to do was turn her head an inch and he would be kissing her mouth instead of her ear. "I was hoping to hear those words when you were naked and lying beneath me."

She grinned and wiggled her bottom against the front of his jeans. Adam was indeed taking her declaration of love hard. Very hard! "I'll keep that in mind for later."

He groaned as he hauled her closer. "Em, you're killing me here."

She giggled. Lord help her, she was a thirty-two-year-old mother of three and she was lying in a man's arms and giggling. "I'm not even touching you." She waited a heartbeat, then added, "Yet."

Adam's loud groan was lost in another chorus of aahs. "Wait until I get you home. I'll give you 'yet'."

She smiled and turned her head that one inch. She wanted Adam to kiss her. No one was paying them any attention. The night sky offered more compelling entertainment. Adam had said, *Wait until I get you home.* He had referred to her house as home. She prayed with all her heart that he had really meant it, because she had one very important question to ask him later.

As the finale raged overhead and cheers erupted all around them, Adam claimed her mouth with a gentleness born out of love.

Two hours later Adam used his last ounce of control to hang on to the edge. He needed Emily to shatter first, and she was precariously close to climaxing. He could feel it in the frantic movements of her thighs as they tried to pull him in deeper. He couldn't go any deeper. He was already touching her soul. Her short nails were digging into his back, but he didn't mind the pain. The little stabs of pain were helping to keep him in control.

He thrust again and watched as she opened her eyes. Green fire. There were no other words to describe the blaze flashing there. The fire consumed him. Emily consumed him, body, mind, and soul. He couldn't hang on much longer. "Now, Em, now," he begged.

A smile teased her lips as she whispered, "I love you, Adam Young."

He captured her mouth and the words just as she shattered in his arms. Her tiny convulsions that trembled and gripped the length of him, buried deep inside her, pushed him over the edge. His hoarse cry of released pleasure mingled with hers.

Adam continued to hold her close long after their breathing returned to normal and their bodies cooled from scalding to glowingly warm. Emily wasn't asleep yet. By her uncharacteristic fidgeting, he would have to guess something was bothering her. He wondered if it was the same thing that was plaguing him.

Now that he had her love, he wanted more. He didn't want to continue sneaking out of her house at the crack of dawn so that the kids wouldn't know he'd spent the night in their mother's bed. Hell, every neighbor on the street knew by now what was going on. How much longer did Emily think they could keep something like this from the kids? He wanted his clothes hanging next to hers. He wanted his own razor in the bathroom, instead of having to use one of her pink plastic disposables with a damn daisy on the handle. He wanted to eat breakfast with her and the kids in her cheery kitchen. He wanted to know she would always be there when he came home. This was his home now. This was where his heart was.

He wanted to get married, and as far as he was concerned, the sooner the better.

He felt her shift away and allowed her to go. Emily was obviously searching for her own answers.

"Adam, do you like children?"

All things considered, it was one hell of a strange question for her to ask. "Whose children? Yours, all children, Mitzi's kids?" Why would she ask about children, unless . . . He glanced at the empty foil package on the nightstand, then back at the sheet that covered her stomach. They had used protection every time they'd made love, but accidents did happen. "Are you trying to tell me you're pregnant?" For the life of him he couldn't figure out why such a prospect made him so damn happy. Emily was carrying his child! A child he never knew he had wanted until this very moment. He wanted Emily to have his child. A child conceived in love.

"Good Lord, no!" The look on her face was pure shock. "I'm not pregnant, Adam."

She didn't have to sound so relieved about it. "Don't you want any more children?" Maybe she'd already made sure she couldn't have any more children. Maybe she'd wanted to use the condoms because this was the nineties and everyone should be practicing safe sex.

"Well, I . . ." She blushed a brilliant red and seemed at a loss for words. "It would have to be under the right circumstances."

"What kind of circumstances?" He was intrigued by the blush and was tempted to pull the sheet away from her breasts just to see what else was such a becoming shade of red.

"A husband." She had to clear her throat twice before she could continue. "A husband would definitely be in order."

He grinned. He couldn't possibly pass up such a golden opportunity. "Speaking of husbands . . ."

She flushed a deeper shade of red and was doing the most peculiar thing with one of her hands. She was making that imaginary gun again and appeared to be shooting it. "Yes, speaking of husbands . . ."

He took a deep breath and quickly interrupted her. "Will you marry me?"

". . . will you marry me?" she continued in unison with him.

Surprised, they looked at each other. When they realized what the other had asked, they both grinned.

Adam hauled her back into his arms and nearly shouted, "Yes." Emily's affirmative reply was crushed under the weight of his mouth.

It wasn't until much later that either of them caught their next full breath. Adam lay totally exhausted across the peach-colored sheets. The only part of his body he could move was his mouth. And it was grinning.

Emily was sprawled across his chest, wondering if they were going to kill each other doing this for the next fifty years. She brushed a damp curl away from her eyes and glanced at Adam. Lord, he was handsome. What had she ever done in her life to deserve a man like him?

Her fingers toyed with the hair on his chest and she smiled. "I guess Jordon is going to get his birthday wish after all."

Adam chuckled and captured her fingers before they started any more trouble. "Wouldn't want to disappoint the boy now, would we? Birthday wishes are very important."

Emily smiled and listened to the rhythmic beating of his heart. "That reminds me, when's your birthday?"

"September the eighth."

Two months away. "Do you know what you'll be wishing for?"

"Well, considering I'll be a married man by then, I think I'll be wishing real hard for my wife to be thinking along the lines of expanding our family."

Emily didn't know what shocked her more, that he wanted to be married within two months or that he was already planning on another child. "Don't you think we should wait awhile?"

He pulled her up his chest until her mouth was poised directly above his. "I've been waiting my whole life for you, Em. Don't make me wait any longer."

How could she refuse such a heartfelt request? She gave him a soft smile. "There's something wonderful about a garden wedding."

EPILOGUE

Emily helped Samantha and Holly out of the van, then turned her attention to the woman emerging from the passenger seat: Adam's mother, Celeste. She hurried around and grabbed the two garment bags before Celeste could. "Thank you, Celeste, for helping me choose the perfect dress and for recommending The White Lace and Promises Boutique. They had just the right selection." Not only had Emily found the most gorgeous butter-cream-colored dress, but she'd found an adorable gown in pale rose for Samantha. Sam's dress was still at the shop being hemmed. She only prayed the child stayed clean during the ceremony.

Celeste took from Emily the bag that contained her own dress. "The boutique came highly recommended, and no thanks are necessary. I enjoyed myself immensely." She turned and took Sam's little hand.

Adam's parents had been a wonderful surprise, Emily thought. She didn't know what she had expected, but they seemed thrilled with the idea of getting not only a daughter-in-law next month but three grandchildren as well. This afternoon's dress expedition had been Celeste's idea, and she had insisted Samantha come too. It was the "girls'" afternoon off, and the men were in charge of the boys.

Emily glanced at the house and prayed everything had gone equally as well for Adam and the boys. "Should we go see how the men are?" She already knew the house was in a shambles. It had been in a shambles before they had left for the store. It had been in a shambles for a week, but Adam promised it would all be put to rights before the wedding. Adam's wedding gift to her and to himself was the installation of central air-conditioning and a new heating system.

They heard the commotion before they opened the front door. Emily managed to give Celeste a confident smile before opening the door and stepping into bedlam. The two women and one little girl stood perfectly still and unnoticed in the main hall.

Adam was carrying Christopher on his shoulders and shouting something about onward and upward as he marched up the stairs. Christopher was banging on his head, yelling, "Pooh, pooh, pooh."

Celeste leaned toward Emily and asked, "Does he have to go to the bathroom?"

"No, he wants his bear, Winnie-the-Pooh." She dismissed Adam and her son and stared in wonder at the sight in the living room. Franklin, Adam's seventy-eight-year-old father, was standing next to Jordon, and they were performing a duet of Elvis's song "Kentucky Rain." Emily was horrified, because she knew what that meant. Elvis had once again escaped his cage.

Celeste looked properly impressed. "He has a wonderful voice, doesn't he?"

"Who, Jordon?" She'd never thought about her son's singing voice before.

"No, Franklin. He used to sing in the shower all the time. I loved listening to him."

Emily wasn't sure she wanted to know any more about what Adam's father did in the shower. If he was anything like his son . . . A blush swept up her cheeks as Christopher's greeting echoed throughout the house. "Mommy home!"

The duet immediately came to a screeching halt. Adam hurried down the stairs and Christopher nearly fell into her arms.

"Thank God you're home," Adam said. "We can't find Pooh."

Emily absently gave Christopher a kiss and set him on his feet. "He's upstairs in my bed, Christopher, right where you left him this morning." The small boy hurried toward the steps.

Adam gave Emily a hard swift kiss before spinning her around in the air. "Lord, woman, I've missed you." The garment bag containing her dress would have fallen to the floor if Celeste hadn't grabbed it.

Celeste shook out the bag and smiled at her son. "She's only been gone a couple of hours."

Franklin and Jordon came into the hall, peering

around the floor. "What are you two looking for?" Celeste asked.

Franklin grinned. "Elvis, my dear."

"Last report has him delivering pizzas in the small rural town of Hog Valley, Idaho," Celeste replied with a straight face.

Franklin took the garment bags from Celeste, hung them on the nearby coatrack, pulled her into his arms and started slow dancing while singing, "Can't Stop Loving You."

Adam followed suit with Emily. Jordon and Sam sat on the bottom step to watch. Christopher and Pooh quickly joined them. Emily glanced over at Celeste and offered an apologetic smile. The poor woman hadn't met Elvis yet.

Celeste returned Emily's smile with genuine pleasure. "What can I say? As you can see, Adam doesn't get it from my side of the family."

THE EDITORS' CORNER

May Day! Cinco de Mayo! Mother's Day! Memorial Day! Armed Forces Day! Okay, okay, that last one's a stretch, but hey, the merry month of May is a time to celebrate. May signals the beginning of summer, National Barbecue Month, picnics, fairs, and don't forget, four excellent LOVESWEPTs knocking on the door. This month's quartet of love includes a stolen dog, a sleepwalker, a man with a smile that should be registered as a lethal weapon, and a woman who picks herbs in the nude! How's that for reading variety?

Take one U.S. marshal, a feisty P.I., an escaped convict, and a stolen poodle, and you've got a surefire way of learning the **TRICKS OF THE TRADE,** LOVESWEPT #834 by Cheryln Biggs. Mick Gentry and B.J. Poydras have no reason to know each other—after all, he's from Nevada and she's from

Louisiana. But the two are destined to meet when his case takes a nosedive straight into hers. The spunky detective prefers working alone, which is just fine with the rugged marshal, but when clues keep leading them to each other, can he convince her to put aside their differences long enough to give love a chance? Cheryln Biggs ignites a sizzling partnership that's hotter than a sultry summer night in the Big Easy!

When Duncan Glendower watches Andrea Lauderdale sleepwalk straight into his bed and into his arms, he realizes that he's a goner in Kathy Lynn Emerson's **SLEEPWALKING BEAUTY,** LOVE-SWEPT #835. Haunted by events that refuse to let her sleep in peace, Andrea reaches out to him in the darkness, tempting him to break all his rules. Struggling to protect the troubled beauty in a remote lodge, Duncan knows that sharing close quarters with the woman he's always loved is risky at best. But can he help Andrea fight the fears that rule her and prove to her that he'll never let her go? Kathy Lynn Emerson explores a man's desire to protect what's precious in this deeply moving novel of passion and possession.

Worried that the deadly threats against her small airport are somehow linked to the arrival of charter pilot Dillon Kinley, Sami Reed must decide if she dares to trust a sexy stranger who is **CHARMED AND DANGEROUS,** LOVESWEPT #836, by Jill Shalvis. Flashing a killer smile and harboring a score to settle, Dillon informs Sami that he won't be an easy tenant to please. But when fury turns to tenderness and old sorrows to new longings, can Sami win her rebel's love? New to LOVESWEPT, Jill Shalvis beguiles readers with a breathless tale of revenge and remembrance about the rogue whose caresses make his cool-eyed spitfire shameless.

In **MIDNIGHT REMEDY**, LOVESWEPT #837, Eve Gaddy brings together a lady with a slightly sinful past and a doctor who's traveled miles of bumpy road to reach her. Piper Stevenson has supposedly cured one of Dr. Eric Chambers's patients with a mystical remedy that she refuses to share. When Eric lights a fire in Piper's heart, will this nursery owner allow herself to come out of the darkness and into the lightness of love? Eve Gaddy reveals a delectably funny and yet touchingly poignant romance that renews faith in the heart and tells of a forgiveness strong enough to last forever.

Pssst! Not to spoil a surprise, but . . . keep an eye out for some changes on the LOVESWEPT horizon when we bring back a new, yet traditional look to our covers!

Happy reading!

With warmest wishes,

Shauna Summers

Joy Abella

Shauna Summers   Joy Abella

Editor   Administrative Editor

P.S. Look for these Bantam women's fiction titles coming in May. New in paperback, **MISCHIEF**, from *New York Times* bestselling author Amanda Quick. Imogen Waterstone has always prided herself on being an independent young woman. Now she needs the help of Matthias Marshall, earl of Colchester, a man of implacable will and nerves of iron. But when the earl arrives, so does a malevolent threat that emerges from London, a threat sinister enough to endanger both their lives. And bestselling author Karyn Monk returns with **ONCE A WARRIOR**, a passionate medieval tale that sweeps you away to a remote fortress in the Scottish Highlands, and the man who must fight to win the heart of his beautiful princess. Ariella MacKendrick needs a hero and she has only a seer's visions to guide her to the Black Wolf, a knight of legendary strength and honor with a vast army. A fire still rages in his warrior heart, but can love transform him into a hero? And immediately following this page, preview the Bantam women's fiction titles on sale *now*!

For current information on Bantam's women's fiction, visit our new Web site, ISN'T IT ROMANTIC, at the following address: **http://www.bdd.com/romance**.

Don't miss these extraordinary
women's fiction titles by your
favorite Bantam authors

On sale in March:
A THIN DARK LINE
by *Tami Hoag*

THE BRIDE'S
BODYGUARD
by *Elizabeth Thornton*

PLACES BY THE
SEA
by *Jean Stone*

When a sadistic act of violence
leaves a woman dead . . .
When a tainted piece of evidence
lets her killer walk . . .
How far would you go to see justive done?

A THIN DARK LINE

the new hardcover thriller
by *New York Times* bestselling author

Tami Hoag

When murder erupts in a small Southern town, Tami
Hoag leads readers on a frightening journey to the shadowy
boundary between attraction and obsession, law and jus-
tice—and exposes the rage that lures people over a thin
dark line.

Her body lay on the floor. Her slender arms outflung,
palms up. Death. Cold and brutal, strangely intimate.

The people rose in unison as the judge emerged
from his chambers. The Honorable Franklin
Monahan. The figurehead of justice. The decision
would be his.

Black pools of blood in the silver moonlight. Her life
drained from her to puddle on the hard cypress floor.

Richard Kudrow, the defense attorney. Thin,
gray, and stoop-shouldered, as if the fervor for justice
had burned away all excess within him and had begun
to consume muscle mass. Sharp eyes and the strength
of his voice belied the image of frailty.

Her naked body inscribed with the point of a knife. A work of violent art.

Smith Pritchett, the district attorney. Sturdy and aristocratic. The gold of his cufflinks catching the light as he raised his hands in supplication.

Cries for mercy smothered by the cold shadow of death.

Chaos and outrage rolled through the crowd in a wave of sound as Monahan pronounced his ruling. The small amethyst ring had not been listed on the search warrant of the defendant's home and was, therefore, beyond the scope of the warrant and not legally subject to seizure.

Pamela Bichon, thirty-seven, separated, mother of a nine-year-old girl. Brutally murdered. Eviscerated. Her naked body found in a vacant house on Pony Bayou, spikes driven through the palms of her hands into the wood floor; her sightless eyes staring up at nothing through the slits of a feather Mardi Gras mask.

Case dismissed.

The crowd spilled from the Partout Parish courthouse, past the thick Doric columns and down the broad steps, a buzzing swarm of humanity centering on the key figures of the drama that had played out in Judge Monahan's courtroom.

Smith Pritchett focused his narrow gaze on the dark blue Lincoln that awaited him at the curb and snapped off a staccato line of "no comments" to the frenzied press. Richard Kudrow, however, stopped his descent dead center on the steps.

Trouble was the word that came immediately to Annie Broussard as the press began to ring themselves around the defense attorney and his client. Like every other deputy in the sheriff's office, she had hoped against hope that Kudrow would fail in his attempt to get the ring thrown out as evidence. They had all hoped Smith Pritchett would be the one crowing on the courthouse steps.

Sergeant Hooker's voice crackled over the portable radio. "Savoy, Mullen, Prejean, Broussard, move in front of those goddamn reporters. Establish some distance between the crowd and Kudrow and Renard before this turns into a goddamn cluster fuck."

Annie edged her way between bodies, her hand resting on the butt of her baton, her eyes on Renard as Kudrow began to speak. He stood beside his attorney looking uncomfortable with the attention being focused on him. He wasn't a man to draw notice. Quiet, unassuming, an architect in the firm of Bowen & Briggs. Not ugly, not handsome. Thinning brown hair neatly combed and hazel eyes that seemed a little too big for their sockets. He stood with his shoulders stooped and his chest sunken, a younger shadow of his attorney. His mother stood on the step above him, a thin woman with a startled expression and a mouth as tight and straight as a hyphen.

"Some people will call this ruling a travesty of justice," Kudrow said loudly. "The only travesty of justice here has been perpetrated by the Partout Parish sheriff's department. Their *investigation* of my client has been nothing short of harassment. Two proir searches of Mr. Renard's home produced nothing that might tie him to the murder of Pamela Bichon."

"Are you suggesting the sheriff's department manipuilated evidence?" a reporter called out.

"Mr. Renard has been the victim of a narrow and fanatical investigation led by Detective Nick Fourcade. Y'all are aware of Fourcade's record with the New Orleans police department, of the reputation he brought with him to this parish. Detective Fourcade *allegedly* found that ring in my client's home. Draw you own conclusions."

As she elbowed past a television cameraman, Annie could see Fourcade turning around, half a dozen steps down from Kudrow. The cameras focused on him hastily. His expression was a stone mask, his eyes hidden by a pair of mirrored sunglasses. A cigarette smoldered between his lips. His temper was a thing of legend. Rumors abounded through the department that he was not quite sane.

He said nothing in answer to Kudrow's insinuation, and yet the air between them seemed to thicken. Anticipation held the crowd's breath. Fourcade pulled the cigarette from his mouth and flung it down, exhaling smoke through his nostrils. Annie took a half step toward Kudrow, her fingers curling around the grip of her baton. In the next heartbeat Fourcade was bounding up the steps—straight at Marcus Renard, shouting, "NO!"

"He'll kill him!" someone shrieked.

"Fourcade!" Hooker's voice boomed as the fat sergeant lunged after him, grabbing at and missing the back of his shirt.

"You killed her! You killed my baby girl!"

The anguished shouts tore from the throat of Hunter Davidson, Pamela Bichon's father, as he hurled himself down the steps at Renard, his eyes rolling, one arm swinging wildly, the other hand clutching a .45.

Fourcade knocked Renard aside with a beefy shoulder, grabbed Davidson's wrist and shoved it skyward as the .45 barked out a shot and screams went up all around. Annie hit Davidson from the right side, her much smaller body colliding with his just as Fourcade threw his weight against the man from the left. Davidson's knees buckled and they all went down in a tangle of arms and legs, grunting and shouting, bouncing hard down the steps, Annie at the bottom of the heap. Her breath was pounded out of her as she hit the concrete steps with four-hundred pounds of men on top of her.

"He killed her!" Hunter Davidson sobbed, his big body going limp. "He butchered my girl!"

Annie wriggled out from under him and sat up, grimacing. All she could think was that no physical pain could compare with what this man must have been enduring.

Swiping back the strands of dark hair that had pulled loose from her ponytail, she gingerly brushed over the throbbing knot on the back of her head. Her fingertips came away sticky with blood.

"Take this," Fourcade ordered in a low voice, thrusting Davidson's gun at Annie butt-first. Frowning, he leaned down over Davidson and put a hand on the man's shoulder even as Prejean snapped the cuffs on him. "I'm sorry," he murmured. "I wish I could'a let you kill him."

The author of the national bestseller *Dangerous to Hold* once again combines intoxicating passion with spellbinding suspense . . .

He'd sworn to protect her with his life.

THE BRIDE'S BODYGUARD
BY ELIZABETH THORTON

"A major, major talent . . . [a] superstar."—*Rave Reviews*

With his striking good looks, Ross Trevenan was one of the most attractive men Tessa Lorimer had ever seen. But five minutes in his company convinced her he was the most arrogant, infuriating man alive. That's why it was such a shock to discover Trevenan's true purpose: hired to escort her out of Paris and back to England, he had sworn that he'd do anything to keep her safe—even if he had to marry her to do it. Now, finding herself a bride to a devastatingly attractive bodyguard seems more hazardous than any other situation she could possibly encounter. Yet Tessa doesn't know that she holds the key to a mystery that Trevenan would sell his soul to solve . . . and a vicious murderer would kill to keep.

A movement on the terrace alerted Ross to the presence of someone else.

"Paul?"

Tessa's voice. Ross threw his cheroot on the ground and crushed it under his heel.

"Paul?" Her voice was breathless, uncertain. "I saw you from my window. I wasn't sure it was you until I saw our signal."

Ross said nothing, but he'd already calculated that he'd stumbled upon the trysting place of Tessa and her French lover and had inadvertently given their signal merely by smoking a cheroot.

Tessa entered the gazebo and halted, waiting for her eyes to become accustomed to the gloom. "Paul, stop playing games with me. You know you want to kiss me."

It never crossed Ross's mind to enlighten her about his identity. He was too curious to see how far the brazen hussy would go.

Her hands found his shoulders. "Paul," she whispered, and she lifted her head for his kiss.

It was exactly as she had anticipated. His mouth was firm and hot, and those pleasant sensations began to warm her blood. When he wrapped his arms around her and jerked her hard against his full length, she gave a little start of surprise, but that warm, mobile mouth on hers insisted she yield to him. She laughed softly when he kissed her throat, then she stopped breathing altogether when he bent her back and kissed her breasts, just above the lace on her bodice. He'd never gone that far before.

She should stop him, she knew she should stop him, but she felt as weak as a kitten. She said something—a protest? a plea?—and his mouth was on hers again, and everything Tessa knew about men and their passions was reduced to ashes in the scorching heat of that embrace. Her limbs were shaking, wild tremors shook her body, her blood seemed to ignite. She was clinging to him for support, kissing him back, allowing those bold hands of his to wander at will from her breast to her thigh, taking liberties she knew no decent girl should permit, not even a French girl.

When he left her mouth to kiss her ears, her eyebrows, her cheeks, she got out on a shaken whisper, "I never knew it could be like this. You make me feel things I never knew existed. You seem so different tonight."

And he did. His body was harder, his shoulders seemed broader, and she hadn't known he was so tall. As for his fragrance—

Then she knew, she *knew*, and she opened her eyes wide, trying to see his face. It was too dark, but she didn't need a light to know whose arms she was in. He didn't wear cologne as Paul did. He smelled of fresh air and soap and freshly starched linen.

"Trevenan!" she gasped, and fairly leapt out of his arms.

He made no move to stop her, but said in a laconic tone, "What a pity. And just when things were beginning to turn interesting."

She was so overcome with rage, she could hardly find her voice. "*Interesting?* What you did to me was not interesting. It was *depraved.*"

The lights on the terrace had yet to be extinguished, and she had a clear view of his expression. He could hardly keep a straight face.

"That's not the impression you gave me," he said. "I could have sworn you were enjoying yourself."

"I thought you were Paul," she shouted. "How dare you impose yourself on me in that hateful way."

He arched one brow. "My dear Miss Lorimer, as I recall, you were the one who imposed yourself on me. I was merely enjoying a quiet smoke when you barged into the gazebo and cornered me." His white teeth gleamed. "Might I give you a word of advice? You're too bold by half. A man likes to be the hunter. Try, if you can, to give the impression that *he* has cornered *you.*"

She had to unclench her teeth to get the words out. "There is no excuse for your conduct. You knew I thought you were Paul."

"Come now. That trick is as old as Eve."

Anger made her forget her fear, and she took a quick step toward him. "Do you think I'd want your kisses? You're nothing but my grandfather's lackey. You're a secretary, an employee. If I were to tell him what happened here tonight," she pointed to the gazebo, "he would dismiss you."

"Tell him, by all means. He won't think less of me for acting like any red-blooded male. It's your conduct that will be a disappointment to him." His voice took on a hard edge. "By God, if I had the schooling of you, you'd learn to obey me."

"Thank God," she cried out, "that will never come to pass."

He laughed. "Stranger things have happened."

She breathed deeply, trying to find her calm. "If I'd known you were in the gazebo, I would never have entered it." His skeptical look revived her anger, and said, "I tell you, I thought you were Paul Marmont."

He shrugged. "In that case, all I can say is that little girls who play with fire deserve to get burned."

She raged, "You were teaching me a lesson?"

"In a word, yes."

Her head was flung back and she regarded him with smoldering dislike. "And just how far were you prepared to go in this lesson of yours, Mr. Trevenan? Mmm?"

He extended a hand to her, and without a trace of mockery or levity answered, "Come back to the gazebo with me and I'll show you."

In the bestselling tradition of Barbara Delinsky, an enthralling, emotionally charged novel of friendship, betrayal, forgiveness and love.

JEAN STONE
PLACES BY THE SEA

Glamorous newswoman Jill McPhearson's past is calling her back . . . to an island, a house, a life she wants only to forget. Putting her childhood home on Martha's Vineyard in order takes all Jill's strength, but it will also give this savvy reporter her biggest break: the chance to go after the story of a lifetime . . . her own.

By the time she reached the end of Water Street, Jill realized where she had come. The lighthouse stood before her. The lighthouse where she'd spent so many hours, months, years, with Rita, thinking, dreaming, hoping.

She climbed down the dunes and found the path that led to their special place. Perhaps she'd find an answer here, perhaps she'd find some understanding as to what she had just read.

On the rocks, under the pier, what she found, instead, was Rita.

Jill stared at the back of the curly red hair. On the ground beside Rita stood a half-empty bottle of scotch. The ache in Jill's heart began to quiet, soothed by the comforting presence of her best friend—her once, a long time ago, best friend. She brushed her tears away and took another step.

"Care to share that bottle with an old friend?" she asked. "May I join you?"

Rita shrugged. "Last time I checked, it was still a free country."

Jill hesitated a moment. She didn't need Rita's caustic coldness right now. What she needed was a friend.

She hesitated a moment, then stooped beside her friend. "I thought maybe you'd be glad to see me."

Rita laughed. "Sorry. I was just too darned busy to roll out the red carpet."

Jill settled against a rock and faced Rita.

"Are you still angry at me for leaving the island?"

Rita stared off toward Chappy. "If I remember correctly, I left before you did."

"Where did you go, Rita? Why did you leave?"

Picking up the bottle of scotch, Rita took a swig. She held it a moment, then passed it to Jill without making eye contact. "Why did it surprise you that I left? You were the one who always said what a shithole this place was. You were the one who couldn't wait to get out of here."

Jill looked down the long neck of the bottle, then raised it to her lips. "But you were the one who wanted to stay."

Rita shrugged again. "Shit happens."

She handed the bottle back. "I've missed you."

A look of doubt bounced from Rita to Jill. "How long has it been? Twenty-five years? Well you missed me so much I never even got a Christmas card."

"My mother never told me you'd come back."

"That's no surprise. You should have guessed, though. You always thought I was destined to rot in this place."

Reaching out, Jill touched Rita's arm. Rita pulled away.

Jill took back her hand and rested it in her lap. "I was trying to make a new life for myself."

"And a fine job you did. So what is it now, Jill? Going to be another of the island's celebrities who graces us with your presence once a year?"

"No I'm selling the house."

Rita laughed. "See what I mean? You don't care about it here. You don't care about any of us. You never did."

A small wave lapped the shore. "Is that what you think?"

"You always thought I'd wind up like my mother. Well, in a lot of ways I guess I did. That should make you happy."

"Rita . . . I never meant . . . "

Rita's voice was slow, deliberate. "Yes you did. You were smarter than me, Jill. Prettier. More ambitious. I guess that's not a crime."

"It is if I hurt you that badly."

"You didn't hurt me, Jill. Pissed me off, maybe. But, no, you didn't hurt me."

Jill remembered Rita's laughter, Rita's toughness, and that Rita had always used these defenses to hide her insecurities, to hide her feelings that she wasn't as good as the kids who lived in the houses with mothers and fathers, the kids with dinner waiting on the table and clean, pressed clothes in their closets.

The heat of the sun warmed her face. "Life doesn't always go the way we want," she said. "No matter how hard we try."

Rita pulled her knees to her chest. "No shit."

The sound of a motor boat approached. They

both turned to watch as it shot through the water, white foam splashing, leaving a deep "V" of a wake.

"I can't believe you still come here," Jill said.

"Not many other places to think around here," Rita answered. "Especially in August." She hugged her knees, and looked at Jill. "I was real sorry about your parents. Your dad. Your mother."

"Thanks."

"I went to the service. For your mother."

Jill flicked her gaze back to the lighthouse, to the tourists. "I was in Russia," she said, aware that her words sounded weak, because Rita would know the real reason Jill hadn't returned had nothing to do with Russia. "Is your mother still . . ."

"Hazel?" Rita laughed. "Nothing's going to kill her. Found herself a man a few years ago. They live in Sarasota now."

Jill nodded. "That's nice. She's such a great person."

Rita plucked the bottle again and took another drink. "Yeah, well, she's different."

Closing her eyes, Jill let the sun soothe her skin, let herself find comfort in the sound of Rita's voice, in the way her words danced with a spirit all their own—a familiar, safe dance that Jill had missed for so long. "I've never had another best friend, Rita," she said, her eyes still closed to the sun, her heart opening to her friend.

Rita didn't reply.

Jill sat up and checked her watch. "I'd love to have you meet my kids," she said. "In fact, I have to pick up my daughter now." She hesitated a moment, then heard herself add, "Would you like to come?"

Rita paused for a heartbeat, or maybe it was two. "What time is it?"

"Five-thirty."

"I've got to start work at six. I tried to quit, but Charlie wouldn't let me. I'm a waitress there. At the tavern. Like my mother was."

"Tell Charlie he can live without you for one night," Jill said. "Come with me, Rita. Please."

Rita seemed to think about it. "What the hell," she finally said. "Why not."

The sun seemed to smile; the world seemed to come back into focus. "Great," Jill said, as she rose to her feet. "We've got so much to catch up on. First, though, we have to go back to my house and get the car. Amy's out at Gay Head."

"The car?" Rita asked.

Jill brushed off her shorts. "Hopefully, the workmen or any of their friends haven't boxed me in. I'm having some work done on the house and it's a power-saw nightmare."

"I'll tell you what," Rita said as she screwed the cap on the bottle. "You get the car. I'll wait here."

Jill didn't understand why Rita didn't want to come to the house, but, then Rita was Rita, and she always was independent. "Don't go away," she said as she waved good-bye and headed toward the road, realizing then that she hadn't asked Rita if she had ever married, or if she had any kids.

She was in the clear. At least about Kyle, Rita was in the clear.

She stared across the water and hugged her arms around herself. Jill had never known why Rita had left the Vineyard; she'd never known that Rita had been pregnant. Her secret was safe for now, safe forever.

And Jesus, it felt good to have a friend again.

On sale in April:

MISCHIEF

by Amanda Quick

ONCE A WARRIOR

by Karyn Monk